ALEX W. BLAND
(ANOTHER BEDTIME STORY
FOR GROWN-UPS)

ALEX W. BLAND
(ANOTHER BEDTIME STORY
FOR GROWN-UPS)

BY
K. L. POORE

Author's Dedication

It must be quite high! After all you spend months and years scribbling away (all the while with a wild hair crawling up the patoot) and really have no clue whether people will like the end result, or even give it a chance. Throw in a trauma (let's say a torn tendon), the 'new' depression, a few old depressions (mistakenly thought to have been dealt with appropriately) and a generally cynical & incredulous outlook towards the spinning globe and how it seems to be wobbling out of control and, well, you get the idea. It takes a storage locker filled of hope and barrels full of dedication to sail out in these stormy seas.

It's time for mutiny!

For Denise, who brightens stormy, unruly seas.

And Evan, John & Jim for supporting the author while he takes time to complete what has been (not HAS BEEN) very time consuming and intense.

George Adams. Thanks for the plugs. Here's one for U.

TABLE OF CONTENTS

An Incredibly Forward by Sir James Chelonia

WHAT KIND OF WORLD IS THIS? AN INCREDIBLY FORWARD

by

SIR JAMES CHELONIA

"Porque?"

I don't know why it came out in Spanish but it's all that I could think of at the time. You see the call was unexpected, unsolicited, and quite unpopular since I was just sitting down to dinner with Carol and her husband and I was afraid that my portion of Mrs. Fowle's famous faux-tortuga soup was going to go toes to roses cold.

"I don't really know a thing about the man," I said in my least dismissive tone.

Which was quite true.

I'd heard mention of a few of his works, "Bright Side of the Sun" in particular, and although those mentions were generally favorable, most of my literary acquaintances (at least the ones whose judgment I would give a modicum of credence) viewed most of his work as being too clever by a half. There was some level of agreement in that they didn't fully enjoy the riddles, puzzles, word play and nonsense for nonsense sake until it was much too late in the day for any of it to matter.

Forward

Meaning by afternoon tea.

"But he knows you Sir James," the man on the other end said, "and he's a true admirer of your work." At least he has good taste.

Louis shouted for me from the dining table and I knew that our little dinner party was all but ruined. It's said that the way to a man's heart is through his stomach and I agree, but only up to the point where his ego is placed somewhere between his oral cavity and his small intestine.

"So what is it that you want of me?" I asked, knowing full well he'd called to solicit a scholarly introduction to a piece of fiction. I sighed, feeling half empty.

"Just your usual scholarly introduction. A few pages of this and that… how he stacks up to so-and-so and where his work fits into today's serious literature, how you came to find out about him, what it is you find so appealing about his wondrous writing style."

"That is going to be difficult," I told him, "since I've never read a word he's written."

"That's not true," he replied with some level of determination in his voice, "why there're over 783,137 in the King James Version of the bible alone!"

I considered this for a second and realized he had me there. If he could have reached through the phone and squeezed I might have dieted in the Roman feather fashion.

"Do you have something for me to read?" I asked, dreading his response would be 'Yes' and the remainder of my weekend would be spent marooned on my davenport mining through another work of treacle laced art by the flavour of the month.

Forward

"Yes! I've got the galleys… I'll sail them right over." He hung up.

When I returned to the dining table I found Carol, and her insufferable husband, chatting loudly about how hard it is to find good help these days. It also seemed they'd broken into my best bottle of Hennessy Ellipse and, judging from the difference between where the volume now rested versus the mark I'd etched into the glass to keep the housekeeper at bay, I could see they'd stunk their way through about two full snifters apiece.

"What do you think, Jimmy?" Louis asked as if we'd been friends since childhood. Actually we have, but I didn't want to go into it at the moment as I was still quite perturbed at his consumption of my dinner.

It was then that the blasted blower rang again.

What kind of world is it in which we live that we are forced to bare these oh-so-heavy telephonic burdens like a speckled tri tone Indian donkey or a giant rat in Sumatra?

"Oh let it go," Louis stated forcefully as though I'd ever heed a word he, or his chattering ferret of a wife, would dare to utter.

It was then I decided I hated the both of them.

I instructed Hargreaves, my butler, to pack up the second course and send the insufferable duo on their way. After a quick round of bowl tossing, a minor struggle over the Hennessey and words too harsh for civilized print I was headed back to my study and the phone.

The caller was revealed to be Edmington Oliver, a local businessman and addle headed bore of enormous proportion. As I was a member of his board of sniveling directors I knew I had to endure whatever meaningless nonsense he was wont to spout.

Forward

"Sir James?"

Idiot.

"This is Edmington Oliver."

Id.

I.

Ot.

"We're having a few issues here at the main office and I believe someone with your vast knowledge and comprehensive understanding of all things business related can help us work through a decidedly difficult issue."

I wanted to give him a sound tongue lashing but his excellent decision to call me first dulled my cat-o-nine-words.

"Can you be here in, say, an hour so you both can get started?"

"Both?" I asked.

"I've invited Admiral Sir Puster Noonington as well."

Noonington? A driveling retard of the most pernicious kind!

"I don't know," I answered, hoping to put a stake in his heart's desire. A few hours with Sir Puster is like drowning for a year in a sea of bloody whimsy.

"Please Sir James, I wouldn't ask—"

It was then the doorbell rang and I saw my out.

"Give me an hour," I told him with a sigh.

He was thanking me profusely as I hung up on him.

Forward

And then Hargreaves announced the man with the galleys. My burden grew heavier by the minute.

I don't know why he chose to drive them over himself but there he was, with one of my finest soup bowls on his head like a crown or kippah and a somewhat soggy brown package beneath his arm crook.

"There're a crazy couple at the front entrance of your estate throwing soup at people... still in the bowl!"

I noticed a piece of silver cutlery sticking out of his coat pocket. "Oh," he added, "and spoons."

I had a sudden realization about where the bulk of my ancestral silver inheritance had been disappearing to all these years.

He held the soggy package out and, unthinking, I took it. I hate it when my incredibly sharp and agile mind is dulled by the activities of a few dolts and rotters.

"Shall we say Monday," he asked hopefully.

I sighed again and rolled my eyes, hoping he would collapse and die in front of me, but he merely smiled, turned and exited.

My afternoon was officially ruined... unless...

"The way to a man's heart is through his stomach and I agree, but only up to the point where his ego is placed somewhere between his oral cavity and his small intestine."

DIANE MICHELLE

Thoughts on Alex W Bland

by

Sir James Chelonia

Alex W Bland is a piece of work and wields English like a sword of language hacking indiscriminately across the page. From the first chapter until the last you will read words in many different orders & formations and in all sorts of contexts. Like the best of Joyce or/and Shakespeare it has a beginning, something of a middle & even an end AND although said ending elicits thoughts of the great comedies of the Hellenic era, and the aforementioned middle stage confrontation owes much to Fitzgerald (Barry, not F. Scott) I would have to place AWB firmly into the camp of some other writer who's name escapes me at the moment but is really quite a rousing good author of great complexity and world renown. Hopefully I'll remember his name by the second edition. The beginning is ridiculous.

With all the wonder of Alice's hole, Bland is literature plain and simple. Originative, grammatical and infectious to the point of being diseased with one of those ugly mind damaging bugs such as Cholera, Typhus, Brautigan or Vonnegut, you'll be thrilled when you finally reach the concluding passage. Behold the new era of literature, when it begins.

Sir James Chelonia, Lord of Piggington GCB GCVO QSO CBE ETC

H

CHAPTER 1NE:
GETTING THE SHAFT

It's a well known fact that a day working at Raw Industries Multinational is twice as long as a day at, let's say, Narwhal's Mega-Mart or Vilehelmet Orallie's entirely too sinister Boot Tongue Corporation. And RAW's employees probably wouldn't mind except it means that the nights are half as short, causing everyone... from the highest salaried third level paper shuffler down to the rawest recruit in "D" basement (testing the latest in RAW materials before their eventual shipment to the Germany, Korea or Viet Nam)... to feel perpetually tired.

Management, naturally, is exempt from this sort of importantly nonsensical rigmarole.

To people outside of the company these experiences appear to be no different than theirs, but that's because the Raw "twice as long days and half as short nights" easily line up with the outsiders "long as long days and short as short nights" and at about eight every morning Raw employees intermingle with these sunny faced outsiders as they all collectively make their way to and from work. There's lots of flashing smiles & highly genic photo ops and everyone's generally content with their situation. And besides, whatever it is the RAWers are doing, they just know it must be very important work.

Alex W. Bland was sprawled out behind his 3/4 scale desk (the desk size for all mid-level potential management candidates) dreaming of a cup of coffee and a better life, in that order. He was feeling a little sluggish after having spent the previous evening burning the midnight oil (as he did every night prior to leaving).

Usually this wouldn't matter a whit but on the previous evening, while moving the oil from the elucubrater to the wickholder, a smudgen had dribbled over the edge and the necessarily unnecessary clean up procedures set him a whole 6 minutes behind schedule. Obviously twice as long plus half as short minus six minutes equals fatigue. Or stated more clearly $2L+(S/2)-6m=IsotopeData(sleep,rest)$.

Now, even though a dribbling smudgen tends to create a lot of smoke and very little fire you'd think a three clang alarm had sounded by the way people began to scurry and midwidget about, looking for ways to regain time which was probably lost forever. Instead, it was merely a "we're running late" warning bell of two clangs and a clap, signaling a minute disaster. The scurriers were almost half smiling as they rushed from their offices and cubicles into the hallways of the thirteen floors that made up the Raw Industries Multinational Headquarters. Anything above two clangs signaled a disaster of many more minutes, something greater than a minute disaster, and although ANYTHING **GREATER** was always thought to be superior by the powers that be (and as such highly desirable), the RAW hallway rushers knew that lesser was much greater under this particular circumstance and sought to increase survivability by diminunizing as they fordled and trundled about, looking for answers to a question that had yet to be asked.

After cleaning up the 36 drippings (roughly 3 drops) of midnight oil, Alex considered just how much time would have to be made up in order for everyone to sleep soundly and get to work on time minus fatigue. He didn't really want to make it up because he thought of himself as being a bull head realist and making this much time up flew in the face of Newtonian reason. Then again, if the whole thing was made up he didn't know what the worry was. "Hmmm," he thought as the air conditioning clicked on.

He crammed page after page of take home work into his satchel (where it would stay 'til morning when, while he munched a plate of scrambled eggs as he scanned his e-mail, it would be transformed into catch up) as the math of the current circumstance danced around his head. "Six minutes of work day doubled, that should be easy," he thought… until it occurred to him that the day minutes had progressed into night minutes and should be halved. Or was it six minutes of work halved that needed to be doubled instead? Would that make it quarters? Three minutes over twelve… "that's a quarter," he thought, meaning everyone would have to give up 15 minutes of sleep and arrive 15 minutes early, or go to bed 15 minutes early and arrive at the regular time.

Meanwhile, not wanting to penalize those who weren't involved in the terrible business of the spilling oil, management realized that any employee who was off that day would need to be called and given the choice of an extra 15 minutes of sleep, although they'd still have to arrive on time, or an arrival time 15 minutes later than the norm (with any extra sleep needing to come out of an upcoming night's allotment). The second choice seemed very agreeable to most until they discovered they'd been given 15 night minutes and they'd all arrived twice as late as they should have. Since they'd arrived during day minutes 8:15 became 8:30 and the bulk of these ungrateful employees would be put on the lay off list for their grossly negligent, and flippant, attitude towards work.

While the list was being compiled and comported to match the inevitability of this dire development every non-management corporate employee was given an official reprimand (one of those ugly ones where a large red notation is placed on your permanent record and causes your head to spin at thirty-three and a third revolutions per minute) for arriving too early, or late, as the case may be… that is, every non-management employee excepting Alex (who had changed his mind about going home and spent the night in his office cleaning the fillient on the elucubrater), and Blanca Gomez, the woman he secretly loved.

His love for her was a great secret that no one knew, and he was that one. It seems he hadn't gotten around to telling himself yet, which, as I'm sure you can guess, complicated things a bit, but he figured he'd get around to it eventually and then he, along with everyone else, would know the incredible secret that he had kept in confidence from himself (maybe the only example of confidence he'd experienced).

He was in love.

Blanca hadn't been reprimanded because that evening, while she sat in her cube fretting over her future (it had recently come to management's attention that she was quite beautiful, much more beautiful than the Chairman's wife, a woman who had paid a healthy sum of money for her beauty), she'd done her own midnight math and the figure she'd come up with was quite perplexing (and caused her to worry even more since it was a figure that was much much much more appealing than the Chairman's wife's). On her third try she'd reached the answer: three, which in actuality was nine or 27. After compounding her formula with day and night measurements the true result was that she arrived back at work before she left, therefore (or 8 as the case may be) she was able to hold the door open for herself and greet herself cheerily as she made her way into the elevator to head down to her third floor office on the following morning.

Each day at 8:05am Alex would drop whatever he was doing (usually just arriving at his desk, which resulted in untold bumps and bruises) and rush to the elevator to get a glance of Blanca as she exited or entered or both. He didn't know why (it was a secret after all) but he did it none-the-less which made it all-the-more confounding. But in the long run he didn't really care, because seeing her made him feel as warm as non-spilt mid-oil burning on a cold December evening.

As mentioned, on this particular Friday morning (not too late in December but not too early Alex was dreaming of coffee and a better life… and not even the odd blue-flag gold star accommodation which was, at this very moment, being written into his personal file (he hoped it was an accommodation with more than one bathroom, even if it was only on paper) could divert him from thoughts that his fellow employees would find strangifying, troutlandish and numbling.

After spending most of the morning looking for a missing right parenthesis from the previous paragraph (it was as lost as time), he was entertaining thoughts about what was wrong in his life and what it would take to leave RAW IM and begin anew. Both thoughts were instantly bored, because he wasn't a very entertaining fellow, but listened intently anyway as war broke out in his brain.

The back of his brain was furious with the front and the right hemisphere with the left. "I just can't take it anymore," he thought.

"Oh give it a rest," the front of his brain responded.

"Heed this warning… all seven of ye," said the third half of his brain (the part that's more rational than the ones that wanted to quit, but much less hung up than the ones that spent too much time considering whether to run or not), "ye give and take will come to nye good. Stay on your side of the pons."

It seemed strange to Alex that the third half of his brain spoke with a decidedly Scottish accent but no more, he told himself, than the fact that his frontal lobe sounded like his mother.

Both fourth halves decided against participation since neither of them could swim and they were having a hard time understanding what the third half was saying most of the time. So, with all these rationales but still starved for adventure, Alex took a pen out of the top drawer of his desk and began to write, without really thinking…

```
Dear Sirs and Madams,

This letter is to tender my
resignation effective as of midnight
tonight. Someone else can burn the oil
for a change.
```

He crumpled the paper and tossed it into the double wide waste basket next to his desk. He wrote again.

```
Yo,

I quit.
```

"That should do it." He folded the paper neatly and slipped it into a crisp white envelope. "Won't they be surprised," he thought as he licked the gummy edge and then sealed it by running his finger roughly over the back. The timing of his thoughts versus the licking and sealing hadn't exactly lined up, so when it went through his head it sounded like this...

"T   H   A   T   S   H   O   U   L   D

D   O   IT.

Perfect!

He placed the envelope on the corner, and edge, of his desk and stared at it. Should he address it? "What's your heading? Which way are you going?" It appeared that it didn't know.

"Hi Alex!"

He looked up to see Blanca, her dark eyes alight, framed by the doorway. It wasn't a decent doorway, it had gotten in a bad jamb many years ago and become slightly unhinged. And what it held against Blanca, and why it had it in for her, wasn't exactly clear (except to the door itself, who saw her openness as a threat to all doors, big and small, around the world), but Alex figured once a little more light was shed on the situation the outer layers of the mystery would fall away and she would be exposed as innocent. A lot more light and she'd be over exposed. This imagining fixed in his head like a developing photograph.

The front halves of his brain made a 'tsk tsk' noise, and the third half said something barely decipherable about a "foosty fud," which set the entire works laughing. Alex blushed, hemmed once, hawed twice, opened the top drawer of his desk and began a futile search for some unknown, and as yet un-invented, office supply.

"We missed you at the elevator," she said softly.

"We?" he thought (because he didn't know she was there twice this morning). "Um, the elevator, yes, hi." He didn't know why he was blushing, but he thought she was the most beautiful woman he'd ever seen. It was now apparent that he'd have to reveal to himself the secret that everyone else knew before he did something incredibly stupid or stupidly incredible. She smiled and it was instantly obvious that the latter was out. Her smile was so illuminating that her eyes dulled by comparison, and it was so perfect in its quizzical wonder, that it made him feel extremely, extremely small.

Very small.

Slowly the desk rose up in front of him. It seemed to be growing. Or what?

"Alex?"

He stretched his neck so that he could see over a manila folder resting on top of the desk. "Hi Blanca. I missed you too. I mean I missed seeing you at the elevator. I mean, I don't know…" and he didn't know. He could never be mean to her, at worst he was just average, which upon further consideration was just about the same. The partially pulled out drawer was now above his head and casting a deep shadow.

"...and down the shaft he fell."

CHRISTOPHER ANDERSON

"I like it when you come see me," she said, and her smile chased the shadows away. Suddenly he wasn't quite so puny, which of course is a small horse that cracks really bad jokes. Slowly he began to rise and he had to duck to miss the drawer.

"Really?"

"Yeah, it's always nice knowing someone, um, thinks of you. Well at least someone as nice as you." The place in his brain where secrets were kept had finally stopped laughing and was now awash in a torrent of activity, all related to organization, distinctive application and great amounts of effort. The phone in his head rang and it was his memory calling. "Hey buddy, I got something you should know." Alex hung up and vowed to call back later. As he smiled at Blanca a calm look spread over her face and he couldn't tell whether it was "happy", or one other 65 expressions that he'd catalogued for the last RAW sales presentation. Although he was no longer shrinking, his spine was still headed in that direction. Why didn't he say something?

"You're very beautiful." Someone in the room said this aloud, and it wasn't her. Alex considered that it was his memory calling again because it didn't like being hung up on. She looked positively demure as she turned a crimson shade of red and now he definitely wanted to see her other 64. It seemed the cat was out of the bag.

As Lujuria the cat tore around the office, clawing at anything within a paw's distance, and mewing like it hadn't eaten in forever, Blanca said, "I didn't know you liked cats." Alex didn't know it either, but the way she said it convinced him that he'd love cats for the rest of his life. It felt like his heart was swelling in his chest and who in the hell let out a bagged cat in his office?

"Love 'em, just love 'em," he told her as he rose from his chair, "love 'em," he added for emphasis. When Lujuria realized that Alex was hunting her she would have none of it and soon anything that could be used as an obstruction loomed large between her and him. As Alex tracked the cat from desk to chair to desk again and then over the double wide waste basket before precarious perching on his satchel he heard Blanca say, "Oh, a letter, would you like me to drop it off for you."

He glanced over just in time to see her pick the crisp white envelope off of his desk. Her blouse, a beautiful white silk thing with four gold buttons up the front and a neckline that was nowhere near the neck, drifted slightly open. He couldn't help but notice the smooth, curving, pizmotality of her breasts. Her presence, there in his office and slightly unwrapped, was like Christmas. He could feel himself growing in other ways. He attempted to act nonchalant (forgetting about Lujuria and her dashing, leaping, and clawing) but it wasn't going to happen. Blanca looked up and caught his sight line. For the first and only time in his life he attempted to dress a woman with his eyes, but it was too late. She realized that her blouse had opened.

"Oh," she said, "oh." She took three quick steps backwards, turned, and disappeared.

"Blanca, wait!" Alex shouted as Lujuria clawed at the cuff of his pants. If he wasn't in such a panic he would have realized he was calling out familiarly to someone who, only a few minutes ago, he could barely look in the eyes. Lujuria attempted to devour the juicy meat attached to his anklebone. He shook a leg out into the hallway.

He could see Blanca as she made her way towards the elevators at the end of the hallway. A short man, who a cruel person would say looked like a mole or a long nosed ferret and an even crueler person would say looked like a mole or a wart, stepped out of an office and shouted "Hey, Bunny, I've got that report for you!"

'Bunny?' Who was this wart nosed ferret of a man who had a nickname for the woman he was soon (probably) to discover he loved. As Alex pushed his way past he read the name on moley mole's door plaque, an ugly yellow rectangle that looked like it was just about to fall off of the wall (He could tell that the gum holding it in place had decayed to the point where there was no choice but to remove it and replace it with a new one).

JOE FISCHER

"Better get that fixed Joe."

Fischer looked either stunned or confused as Alex passed. "We can't have—" He didn't finish his thought… he noticed a small gold button lying on the floor. It wasn't really lying but it wasn't being truthful either. He knelt, picked it up and cupped it lightly in the palm of his hand.

"I think that's Bunny's," Joe said with a hint of a lisp.

"Now how would you—" Alex didn't finish this thought either. It was Joe. It was unfortunate. It was his nose. It was long. Preternaturally long. And there, perched on the end, was a gruesome black and purple mole… complete with a single 2" strand of hair poking out of its peak.

"Uh huh," Alex answered. Joe spoke some more but Alex didn't hear a word. He was focused on the hair.

"Will you make sure she gets it?"

"Uh huh," Alex answered.

"Will you give it to her?"

Alex couldn't be sure, but it seemed as if the hair on Joe's nose was its own sentient creature. It would sway slightly, periodically dipping to one side or the other, before standing up as straight as a soldier and snapping off a follicle end salute. Alex was captivated.

"This report?" Joe asked again.

"Uh huh," Alex responded as he snatched the paper from Joe's hand. The hair saluted again and Alex turned and ran towards the elevators.

Closed. The doors were closed. The little red numbers were climbing. Upwards. Upwards. And now down. Down. Down. Alex was excited. She was coming back. No. Not stopping. Down. Down. Down. Ding. The bell sounded. Alex scratched his head with the edge of the paper and waited. "Come on," he thought. Ding. Nothing. "Come on!"

The doors opened and he rushed in...

...and

    down

        the

           shaft

              he

                 fell.

E

CHAPTER 2WO:
A POOL OF SECRETARIES

"Confounded and conflustered," Alex thought.

He had to admit to himself he was both of these things. So much so, in fact, his memory had temporarily stopped trying to explain to him that he was in love with Blanca.

He wasn't really confused by most of the circumstances surrounding the opening of the elevator doors because, although quite curious, they (the elevator doors) seemed to open everyday. "Seemed," he thought, because he couldn't account for those days when he skipped the elevator and took the stairs. Most is a very powerful word when contextually combined and used in concert with confusion. Most is very flustrating.

That the elevator appeared to pass him by prior to stopping was mildly confusing... at most.

That there was no car behind the doors and that he'd fallen into the shaft was very confusing... at most.

His 'extremely confused' flag rose straight to the top of the pole because he'd always believed that he worked on the bottom floor of RAW Industries.

But none of those things were confounding.

What was confounding was that he was still falling… falling so far, and for so long, that he seemed to be going sideways. "So much for elevating," he thought. "I guess that explains most of my bottom floor confusion… but what about the 'mildly' and 'very' aspects of it all?"

As he fell… (Is it falling if you're going sideways? Does that make it sidling?) As he sidled through the darkness he periodically heard shouting, which was invariably followed by splashing noises.

He grew tired of his sidling until, at last, or at penultimate (since there's no way this amount of sidling can last), he found himself standing outside a pair of large white double doors. He chuckled because he had always believed people only found themselves at ashrams, retreats, or in uncomfortable circumstances. A sign on the left door read 'NO' and one on the right read 'ENTRANCE'. So, being expert at following directions and having a clear understanding of the English language, he pushed open the right door and entered.

As he passed through the portal he was confronted by all manner of strangeness and charm. Bright lights flashed and moved, sometimes following each other, sometimes appearing seemingly out of nowhere. Colorful pieces of paper of all shapes and sizes drifted through the air as if a homecoming parade had been going on for 2 or 3 hours. Some pieces were as small as notebook paper, some as large as confetti. A massive rectangular bathing pool, surrounded by a deck of green baize, took up most of the space which was still large enough to hold 3 or 400 women.

Alex figured it had to be closer to 400 because there were 3 women standing within only a few yards of him. The 400 were as varied in shape and size as the paper that danced through the air and most were not wearing very many clothes. 'Very many' meaning none. Alex blushed at his own flustration.

Once he composed himself (something along the lines of Beethoven's 2nd or 4th) he slowly made his way towards the 3. Slowly because, seeing he was the only male in a room filled with 400 women wearing very many clothes, he was unsure if he was supposed to be there, or how they would respond to his presence. If only he had presence like Blanca they'd surely open up and be put at ease.

The first woman was an odd looking bird with multicolored hair that shot out in a multitude of directions and eyes that seemed to be looking in three or four directions at the same time. She held an old timey Rudy Vallee megaphone in her left hand and periodically lifted it to a mouth that was so crooked it looked like she was only talking out of the left side of her head. She shouted at the 397 others.

"There's a rumor going around that some of us are naked. As you know, this is a complete fallacy and an attempt to lower morale. I'm telling you straight up that morale couldn't get any lower! And anyway, isn't it obvious that I am at this very moment addressing you in close proximity. We are all in close! So please disregard these vicious lies."

She held an hourglass wristwatch up to her traveling eyes and watched a few grains of sand tip tip tip into the bottom chamber. She dropped her arm and shouted, "Hold on, it'll just be another minute or so, hold on, just another minute or so." She smiled, held her breath for a few seconds, held up her hourglass wristwatch again and shouted, "Just another 10 minutes! 10 minutes!"

"Excuse me," Alex said to her, "but exactly where are we?"

"Where are we?"

"Yes."

"Yes? That's strangely charming, I thought we were in No! If we're in yes, it changes everything for the better!" And with that she shouted into the megaphone, "Excuse me everyone but this person has just convinced me that it will be another..." she held up her hourglass, "...15 or 20 minutes."

She returned her attention to Alex, "Yes?"

"I was wondering where we are."

"But now you're not because you just told me we're here in Yes!"

"No... that's not correct", he answered.

"Exactly. I always dreamed of going to yes when I was but a wee one... and now here I am. Yes, what a beautiful place!" she replied and returned to her megaphone. "Only seven or 10 minutes. Seven or 10."

One of the other two, a woman who looked like a malnourished weasel with a bad popberry rash around her face, walked up to Alex and said, "I don't think you are supposed to be here. No?"

The first woman said, "No! Yes!"

The second woman quietly muttered, "Don't you know better than to ask a lot questions?" ("No, better?" the first woman said, "I don't think so!) "Don't you worry people might think you're a reporter or something even less desirable?" Her lips were pursed like she'd been sucking on a lemon for 2 or 5 hours and only now had gathered the strength to remove it from her weasely mouth. There were large tufts of hair missing from the top of her head and every so often she would reach up to check to see if some had either grown back or fallen out. She took Alex by the arm and led him away from the bird woman.

"Where is here?" he asked weasely.

"Here is where with a big W missing, don't you think?" She responded. It seemed that everything here was a question in which there were no answers, only more questions.

"Do you know where we're standing?" Alex asked, more flustration creeping in.

"Either right here or in good, as far as I know. In good? Oh does that mean we're no longer in yes? What shall we do? Ask Matty!" With that she turned and shouted, "Matty, where are we?" Matty, a crumply badger with a shock of white hair on top of a doughy head, looked over and said, "I'm not paying attention to you, but if I were I'd say where… here, with a big W out front. Now I'm not saying another thing until Judy tells me who said our proximity clothes were missing."

"Only a few more minutes," Judy shouted through her megaphone as she stared at Matty who, in turning, glared at the other 397.

Alex decided to ask one of the other 397 where he was and walked towards the closest of them, a statuesque beauty painted white with a red stripe running around her body. For a moment Alex forgot about Blanca.

"Excuse me," he said to the woman. She turned and faced him and he forgot about Blanca completely. "Yes?" she replied.

Judy shouted, "I told you so! We're in YES!"

Alex couldn't help but stare at the large white 11 that was painted on the red stripe that ran around her stomach. At least it appeared as if he was staring at the 11. "Where are..." But he didn't have an opportunity to complete his question because the lemon sucking woman fell against Alex who fell against 11 (which he really didn't mind) who then fell into an assortment of women who were standing around chatting and filing their nails. After a few tumbles, crambles and head clackings one of the woman (with a large 14 painted on a green stripe that ran around her body) fell in to the pool.

The lemon mouthed skinny weasel popberry rash woman grabbed him by the arm. "Do you realize that you're not listening to me?" she said

"Yes."

Judy shouted, "That's the place!"

"You haven't said anything worth listening to," Alex added.

"That's just plain ridiculous, everyone listens to me."

With that she turned and looked out at the other women. Only the women painted solid yellow were paying attention.

"What are you doing in the secretarial pool anyway?" She asked angrily.

"Secretarial pool? When did we get a secretarial pool?"

"We is a relative term don't you think? My brother and sister and me, maybe, but you, you're not part of we."

"But this isn't a secretarial pool!"

"It isn't? It seems to be functioning quite well to me." There was a splash and Alex turned to see another unlucky woman (13) fall into the water. Alex started to respond but she said, "I knew that you'd agree."

"We're not in agreement."

"I know that," she replied, "because not more than 5 minutes ago you said that we're in yes. You're a very flustrated, confused, and redundant person."

"Yes is not a place!"

"Well you better tell them," she said, waving her right arm towards the 397, "because they seem to like it here." Alex looked around and every one (since they were already paying attention) seemed to be enjoying what ever it was they were doing.

"Don't secretaries take dictation, shorthand etc…," he asked.

"Shhh, don't say that too loud, you want to hurt their feelings?"

An angry electric hum filled the air and loud speakers surrounding the pool squelched into life. A voice boomed out. "It's an important day for all of us. Our take over of International Fifteen Holders LTD, formerly known as Ménage A' Triangle Very LTD, will be completed later today and then we'll be able to manage them until their old management can come up with a plan that will allow us to leave them successfully on their own to manage themselves. You're all very excited about these circumstances, and even though you'd like to celebrate we're going to wait until after tonight's oil burning. Don't forget to rejoice on your way home. God bless us, and God bless the CEO."

"NOW!" shouted Judy and a group of non-painted women furiously filled large RAW logo'd jugs with water from the pool. Once full, they took 10 synchronized steps to the left, 20 exacting steps to the right, 10 delicate steps to the left, and then poured the water back in. Judy looked over towards Alex and the lemon faced woman and said, "Aren't we just fantastic Michele?"

"Yes, Judy." Michele responded.

Judy smiled and said, "That's the place," before frowning at Matty.

"A family squabble," Michele said to Alex as if that would explain the obvious animosity between Judy and Matty.

"Does the CEO address you like that often?" Alex asked her.

"Never! But he subdresses us a few times a day."

The loudspeaker system squelched and CEO spoke again. "By the way, I'm looking for Alex W Bland, anyone seen him?" And he clicked off. Judy shouted "NOW," and once again the unpainted ladies of the secretarial pool performed their task. Upon seeing this the painted ones began running into each other at full tilt, some flopping into the pool, some falling to the ground and spinning.

"Who in hell is Alex Bland," Michele said aloud to no one, and the women not paying attention responded, "Who knows?"

Alex didn't say anything because he knew who in here he was and whatever the CEO wanted, it couldn't be good. Blanca couldn't have delivered his resignation already?

"MY RESIGNATION!"

The color slowly drained from his face as he thought about what he'd done. As if it were happening on cue.

"You look like Dublin circa 1500!" Michele said and Alex knew he'd have to fortify himself in order to continue.

He stood as tall as his 5' 10" would stretch and asked, "Why is there a secretarial pool?"

"Remember when the CEO started at RAW?" Michele asked him.

"Yes."

Judy shouted, "That's the place!"

"Well," Michele continued, "he likes secretaries even less than reporters. Said we get in the way. So he asked the company's best administrative assistants to come up with something new for us. Judy came up with that…" and she looked towards the water women, "and Matty came up with…" and she looked towards the numbered women. "Understand?"

"Not really," Alex answered.

She whispered, "We were never really secretaries at all, we were newspaper reporters and we were afraid we'd be found out. So we closed our eyes, put our hands over our mouths and hoped for the best. It's not that bad a gig if you keep your head down, your teeth clinched and eyes shut."

There was an awful squawk and Alex looked over towards Matty who, it turned out, was its source. She was doing a silly dance that involved bending over, opening her mouth and shouting (that COULDN'T be singing) in a high pitched whine.

Scrambled Eggs,

We need toast and jam and marmalade

You could eat some with us if you stayed

A big ol' plate of scrambled eggs!

"What's she doing?"

"Matty? It sounds like the scrambled eggs song. She's been on a diet for a really long time."

"But why is she singing to me?"

"Everyone else has heard it a thousand times." The women who were paying attention nodded their heads.

"She's the worst singer I've ever heard. Why doesn't someone stop her?"

"She's risen to her level of incompetence. It's the perfect job for her. Those that can't do, do."

"That's what it sounds like. How can you let this happen?"

"Well if she was a good singer some other company might hire her and then we'd have to find someone else. Oh Oh! Cover your ears, here comes another one." Matty squinched her face up into a tortured cinnamon twist and started in on her song & dance again.

Eating is easy if you hold your nose

And you can eat what you don't see

Sometimes I'm starving but that just makes me hungrier

Strawberry Jam

Forever!

"What was confounding was that he was still falling...
falling so far, and for so long, he seemed to be going sideways."

KEN RUGG

"If I hear one more of her songs I might die," Alex shouted as Matty started in on another verse. Right on cue Judy shouted, "Time for lunch everyone." Some one complained, her yellow body turning almost golden in hue. "'sonly 8:45!" A murmur went up among the workers who were paying attention.

Alex knew he'd have to get out of here soon or risk more singing. "Do you know Blanca Gomez?" he asked.

Matty's eyes lit up and she walked towards them. "Fourth floor or third floor Blanca?" Michele asked.

"Third floor Blanca."

"Sorry, never heard of her."

"But…"

"Fourth floor Blanca came through here a few minutes ago."

Judy walked over to join the conversation. "I'm still not taking to you," Matty told her.

"That was third floor Blanca," Judy said.

"It was?" Matty and Michele said in unison before looking at each other and saying, "I'm not talking to you now."

"Of course it was, fourth floor Blanca's the one that likes the midnight oil guy."

"No she's not," Matty replied before Michele finished her sentence with, "that's third floor Blanca."

"Really?" said Alex.

"Really?" said Judy.

"Of course!" answered Matty and Michele before adding, "we are not talking."

"Third floor Blanca?" Alex asked.

"So which one was it?" Judy asked.

"Either three…" said Michele, "or four," finished Matty.

"Stop…" "That!"

"Right…" "Now!"

And Michele and Matty began tugging at each other's clothes. Judy jumped into the fray and soon it was a full-fledged brawl. The numbered ladies slowly drifted over and would have watched the proceedings but a woman who was painted white fell against an 8 who tumbled into the pool and a large segment of the numbered women screamed "we quit!" while all of the other colorful ladies gathered together for a break.

The women by the water waited impatiently to be told what to do. Michele tugged at Matty's hair and soon an ugly wig came off. Matty was a man! And bald! A shriek went up and soon the numbered ladies were covering themselves and attempting to hide behind Alex.

"What are you doing?" he asked a 10.

"Matty's a man, and we're fully exposed!"

"But I'm a man too," Alex said nicely.

An air raid of screams went off and the naked and fully exposed women ran for cover.

"Alex?"

Alex looked up to see Blanca, with her hand to her mouth, on the other side of the pool. She looked at the naked numbered women running around, blushed, and took off running.

Alex sighed and followed after her.

CHAPTER 3HREE:
CAUCASIAN RACE
&
THE MISSING TALE

Alex bolted from the pool area doing his best to avoid the Rainbird level of splashing and, more importantly, clinched fist pummeling that the 397 were attempting to administer him. Merely "his best" because said attempts were proving quite fruitful and their unbridled fury of knuckles and water, which had recently been heaped upon Matty, Michele and Judy (who, it turns out were all men: Matthew, Michael, and Judy), was now reigning down on his head and shoulders like bad orange cheese on ballpark nachos.

As Alex bobbed & weaved his way through the gauntlet mix of raging women and chlorinated baptism towards the doors he'd seen Blanca enter, he felt as if he was an actor in a boxing movie being filmed in high contrast slow motion. The bits of paper which earlier had danced in the air now hung suspended like a colorful paper-maché sky and the noises emitting from the angry women's mouths sounded deep, extended, and mushily bullish. Thousands of bright beautiful lights flashed around him and Alex feared they were the result of far too many shots to his easy to hit melon over the last 16 to 25 feet.

As he reached the doors (which strangely enough had the title of a Jean-Paul Sarte play printed across them) a green woman with a large 6 on her belly punched him behind the right ear and shouted, "You're not getting away that easy!" "Easy?" raced through his head just as he did the same through the Sarte doors, slamming them shut behind him in a single motion. He barely had time to snap a sliding door lock into place before the surging forward line of the 397 began pounding and shouting for the opportunity to wail on his now lumpy head for a while longer.

Alex grimly wondered why it had taken them so long to figure out he was a male. His mind wandered through this minefield of self-esteem until he was distracted by a single, explosive, "whoops!" This "whoops!" was followed by many many falumphing bonks, clacks and pool splashes. And then all became quiet. He listened intently to the silence for a minute or so before turning from the Sarte doors to try and figure out exactly where here was. W or not. He reached into his pocket and rolled the gold button between his fingers as he studied his surroundings.

It was a hallway, four feet wide and painted in reds & black. It was decorated with garish art, lewd paintings (of JC 'Cool' Ledge, John 'UnFinnigan' Morgan and Tommy 'TweedleDee' Lorenzo among many) and an unappealing lifelike half torso statue of Pope John VIII in ornate papal regalia and a peculiarly spotty beard.

The hallway led directly onto a stairway that, as he considered everything about it, caused a feeling of dread to spread over him like a black hood. For a moment he considered unlatching the doors and taking his chances with the now splashing and laughing women of the secretarial pool. Maybe they'd already forgotten about his intrusion! But then he thought about poor Blanca making her way past this creezy stuff and up those stairs to wherever they led and he knew he had to go forward. And up. He didn't fully understand why he cared so much, or at all (come on memory, isn't it time to get with it?), but he decided to plunge ahead into the tasteless creepiness and make sure she was okay. He took a deep breath (maybe three) and walked to the foot of the stairs.

He took a single step up… and found himself at the bottom again. Another step, same result.

He frowned. He leapt up to the second step.

Now he was at the bottom but a full stride further away from the stairway.

"What in hell?" he thought.

He turned to his left and quickly sidled up the first few steps thinking if it worked in the elevator shaft maybe it'd work here. Instead, he was suddenly halfway down the hallway facing the bust of John VIII.

"Name?" Pope John said in a high-pitched voice.

"Beg your pardon," Alex said politely.

"Name?" John restated in a lower tone.

"Alex W. Bland"

"And the double V?"

Alex was puzzled until he realized what he was being asked. "Uh, Wonder… my folks loved the song 'Fingertips (Pt. 2)'."

"What race do ya want ta be in?"

"Sorry?"

"No need ta feel sorry, just want ta know race, boy, race! I haven't got time for indecisiveness." The Pope's voice was very shrill.

"I'm not sure I understand."

A rolling of eyes and a smooth, boney finger was pointed at a sign hanging behind him on the wall. Alex was fairly certain it wasn't there a minute ago. It read, "HUMAN RACE HORSES."

"I'm not a horse," Paul said succinctly.

"Ya don't look very human either but I still got a job ta do. Which race?"

He noticed a large oil painting behind the pope of men in sailor caps swabbing a deck.

"Okay... Boat?"

"No such thing." Thing was pronounced 'ting.'

Next to it was the smiling face of the cartoon character, Raygun Ron riding a laser beam towards the earth.

"Arms?" he asked.

"Nope."

He thought for a second. "Caucasian?"

"REALLY?" Pope John's demeanor changed noticeably, "ya qualify?"

"I'm pretty sure. My mother was Irish and my father was Northern Irish."

"Mix marriage huh? Well, I guess ya qualify. Here's yer Kipling," and with that he handed Alex a book of poetry, "here's your jar of mayonnaise, and here's your official R1B1C6 identity card.

Alex held these things close to his chest and turned towards the stairs.

"Now which level?" Pope John VIII asked him.

Alex rolled his eyes and turned back to him. "Level?"

"I got to know if you can compete, you know. keep up with the big dogs."

A picture of a group of dogs playing poker began to bark wildly.

"Shut it!" the Pope screamed and they quieted immediately.

Alex stared and didn't speak a word.

"Okay," PJ said, "there's the Tyro level, so named because if you don't have a lot of experience that's how you feel at the end.

"I've got years of experience."

"You mean yers of experience."

"Uh, I don't know."

"Who do ya believe has more experience being you?"

"Me?"

"That's right and it's all yers. Therefore you've got yers of experience."

"Well I'm not completely satisfied with my life so far, what else is there?"

"Then there's Mean. I can tell that's not for you because even though yer pleasant I can't for the life of me understand whatever yer getting at."

"I'm just..."

"Perhaps, but that's probably for someone else to decide. I'm here to get ya into the proper category, and since there's only one remaining would ya please step across the hallway. Next!"

With that a bell tinged (which, strangely enough went THING!) and the Pope said, "There's people waiting. Move on. Next!"

Alex turned and walked across the hallway to a painting titled RAT. It consisted of a bed of straw, a piece of cheese, and a carving knife. No rat though.

A "Pssst," sissed from the painting next to it, "Psssst."

Alex peeked over. It was entitled MEISTER.

It was surreal painting of an extremely homely artist with a toothbrush moustache working on a portrait of a huge, entirely red, eagle holding a very, very, small gray rat in its talons. Floating in the sky nearby was a diamond shaped kite in the most exquisite shades of tangerine and marmalade. The "Pssssst" was coming from the rat.

"You think you can give me a hand here?" the rat asked.

"Uh, I'm not sure."

"Come on buddy, I'm not even supposed to be in this picture."

"Really? Then how did you end up in this situation?"

"Oh," the rat said, "it was just awful bad luck, you see I was…" and at just that moment an incredibly strong breeze blew through the story and caught hold of the kite, blowing it clear out of the chapter. And where a kite blows, the tale is sure to follow, so the rat's tale blew all the way into a later chapter.

"Um," Alex said not knowing what had happened but reasoning a guess, "that's tough luck."

"What do you mean?"

The eagle looked at him and frowned.

"You know, caught by an eagle?"

"Eagle?" The rat said and he shuddered. "Where?"

"Ah, you're in his... um..."

"I have no idea what you're talking about."

The eagle spoke up, "Mind your own business!"

"Who said that?" the rat asked.

"Not me," said Alex.

"Not me," said the Red Eagle.

"Not me," said the artist (Who's name happened to be Chicken L. Groover).

"Well someone had to say it."

"Not really," the Red Eagle replied, "No one has to say nothing if they don't want."

As Alex attempted to break this reply down into something he could understand the rat became agitated and screamed at the artist. "I knew it, you lied to me again!"

The artist turned to Alex. "Well thank you very much," he said, "I half worked very hard on this only to half you ruin everything."

"Sorry, I guess," Alex responded.

"Can I eat now?" the Red Eagle asked.

"Of course not," the ugly artist replied, "If you eat him then I'll have nothing to represent the people. How 'bout if I paint you a nice crow?"

"This is supposed to be some kind of representational art?"

"Next to it was the smiling face of the cartoon character, Raygun Ron"

PAT BARR

"Of course it is!" said the Red Eagle.

"Then what do you represent?" Alex asked.

"The most noble of all creatures, struggling to bring food to the co-op."

"Why are you red?"

"Red!" shouted the rat, "that explains a lot."

"Red! I'm supposed to be tricolor!" the Eagle screeched.

Alex looked at the artist.

"He represents a danger people can't see but is there none the less. Boiling beneath the surface. Ever present."

"That's not what you told me!" the Red Eagle cawed.

The rat added, "He said I was the world's first flying mouse."

"If I told you the truth would you let me paint you?" the artist asked the eagle.

"Of course not, you think I like being monochromatic?"

"So you see," the artist stated, "if I told this disposable rodent and unreasonable bird the truth my painting would be finished! It's for the greater great."

"But if they're representations in a representative painting," Alex asked, "that's inside a representative composition then do you represent a style which must lie three deep in order to express its goals?"

"No, I only represent myself. Can't you tell that it is a portrait of a man in a state of Flux."

"Flux… isn't that where Art was promoted to oppress the weak and helpless?"

"Absolutely not. Art would never do such a rank thing! Besides, he doesn't have time to waste on people who can't stand up for themselves."

"Oh wait, Flux is where you are taught to use broad and unflattering strokes!"

"Oh you don't get it at all," the artist told him, "it's strikingly apparent that you are obviously inferior and not a member of the Fluxian school. What is it about your type that allows you to think you can criticize what you'll never truly understand? When Art took over the school it was in disarray… and now look where we are! Very arrayed. Everyone completes their work on time and you never hear any complaints."

As the ugly artist said this he used his paintbrush to point up the stairwell (dripping red all over the floor as he did so).

```
        A
      DROP
    OF RED
    ON THE
     FLOOR
     ISN'T
       BAD
        !!
        he
        sa
        id
        to
        Al
        ex
        wi
        th
        an
        ug
        ly
        gr
        in
         .
```

Alex glanced at the portrait and both the eagle and rat had disappeared. For a moment he was concerned that the artist had painted them out, but then he leaned into it and, faintly against the painting's horizon, he could see a blot of red, with a touch of grey in its beak.

The artist, seeing Alex's distant gaze, looked back to his work and he too noticed they were gone.

"Now look what you've done," he said, "they've gotten away!"

"If only it was that easy," Alex said.

"Now I'll have to start over," the artist said as he reached for his palate. He began with small movements but soon was slashing across his canvas with long wild strokes. He noticed Alex and asked "What did you want, anyway?"

Alex realized he'd been grimacing as he watched the artist viciously attack his work. His face went slack and he answered, "Oh um yeah. I'm in a race of some sort."

"Really. Seems you've lost already."

The artist looked at his painting and his shoulders dropped. "I'm going to need some help," he said loudly before shouting, "Oh Quiz ling ling!"

A portrait of a panda bear in a Viking helmet shouted, "Coming meister!"

Alex took a step backwards and watched. The artist abandoned his previous concept and, with help from the Panda Viking, began painting the earth in the same blacks and reds as the hallway. Alex stepped forward, took the painting down, and turned it so that it faced the wall.

"Hey," shouted the artist, "what are you doing? I can't see!"

Alex smiled as he slowly backed away from the painting. He new better than to turn his back on it so he kept going until he had reached the bottom step… and suddenly he was three steps up from the ground floor. Another step back and he was six. Another, and nine. And Twelve. He took one last step and found himself floating slightly above the top stair, before crashing to the floor.

He picked himself up, dusted himself off, and turned to see where he was now. He was standing at the doors of a large glass room.

Los Prevenciónes

was painted on one of the doors in big black letters. Behind it he could see 10 or 13 men wearing black patches over their left eyes.

He entered as quietly as he could.

CHAPTER 4OUR:
BLANCA
&
THE GLASS CEILING

Alex.

That's all that can be said about his entrance into the glass room because he was attempting to be as quiet as possible. Anything more would surely have drawn attention to him. He noticed a piece of notebook paper on the floor and he bent down and picked it up. It was a memo addressed to Blanca and he unconsciously stuffed it into his shirt pocket and quietly made his way across the room.

"Wow, will you look at that," said the largest of the men, sitting in front of a computer screen. Alex noticed he was the only one in the room with a patch over his right eye.

"What?" said the man standing directly behind right eye.

"What?" said the man to the left of right eye.

"That woman in the lunch room!" shouted the man to the right of right eye.

"What lunch room?"

The man to his left lifted his eye patch and said, "Oh it's on the other side, everybody switch!"

They all tugged their patches over to the other side of their face. A few said, "Ohhhhh, her!" but the largest of the men said, "Now where'd she go?"

"What are we supposed to be looking at," said the man directly behind the man at the terminal.

"The woman in the lunch room. Her... right there."

"But WHAT about her is so important?"

There was a bit of grumbling until one of them said, "Is she supposed to be doing that?"

"Eating her lunch?"

"NO, THAT!"

With that they all moved closer to the screen and stared intently.

The woman was eating her lunch.

"Very suspicious if you ask me," said the tallest man.

"Me too!" said the shortest, who couldn't really see the screen since he was standing directly behind the tallest.

"What?" said the largest.

"Let's have somebody pick her up."

"Like for a date?" said the shortest.

"No not like a date, for an interrogation!"

"And then we'll fire her."

"For theft!"

"And not paying attention."

"And eating with her mouth open."

"She's not eating with her mouth open."

"But she might!"

There was a murmur of agreement before the shortest said, "And I think she's selling secrets to our competitors."

"I think she's buying secrets from our competitors," said the tallest.

"I think she's stealing secrets from one competitor and selling them to another one in order to use the money to secretly make plans to steal secrets from us."

"That's treason!"

"No," said the largest, "I call it Reason with a T. Treason is when someone intentionally inflicts damage upon our corp's ability to monitor our competitor's plans in order to cover up some stupid thing we've done or said or done said."

"That would be totally lame with a P!"

"I don't understand, but you're right!" said another.

"What?" shouted the largest.

"Thank goodness no one at RAW would be dick enough to do something so evil and stupid."

"Here, here," all of the others shouted.

When one of the men shouted a third "Here" everyone turned to him.

"…look… she's gone," he said as the others went into panic mode.

"Ring the alarms, set off the bells, sound the pennywhistles!"

Everyone (except Alex of course) grabbed a pennywhistle from a nearby table and ran goosey loosey around the room, blowing into it while yanking its magic ring out and back.

Whoooooop. Whoooooop.

…went the noise as they scrambled back and fro, to and forth, banging against each other like misshapen balls on a billiards table. Eventually one of the men (sweating profusely) realized if they ran in a circle they wouldn't clank into each other. After a few seconds convincing, they were going around and round and round and round, except for the shortest man who slipped and fell in the profuse man's overabundant sweat.

And that's when the tallest of them noticed Alex tippy toeing towards the rear exit.

They stopped running.

"Who are you and what do you want?"

"Why are you here and what do you want?"

"When did you arrive and what do you want?"

"What do you want and uhh," now they were all perplexed.

"What?" shouted the largest without turning to look.

"Hi, my name's Alex and I saw someone I know come through here." Alex handed his R1B1C6 identity card to the closet one.

As the man slipped the card into his shirt pocket he said, "We know what your name is Axel. We've been keeping an eye on you! No one's been through here."

Alex held up the memo. "Her name's Blanca and she's…"

"Blanca!" shouted the largest before turning three shades of white and fainting.

The others scrambled about until the tallest of them returned with a glass of water and poured it on the formerly largest but now merely fainted one. When the fainted man came to (once again becoming the largest) he said, "I thought you said Blanca…" and at that his eyes rolled up in his head and he passed out again.

"You've got to stop doing that," shouted the smallest.

"But I didn't," Alex offered, "at least not the second time.'

"Are you calling me a liar?" the smallest man quizzed. The others joined in with a chorus of 'he certainly is's' and 'absodamnlutelys'.

"Well let's see how you like this!"

And with that the smallest man in the room made his way to the terminal and typed in AXEL.

The computer hummed and whirred for a second and then made a sound that went Thiinnnnngggggggg.

The smallest man turned and said, "So you're the infamous Axel Crumpweldenstapher! We've been waiting to get you down here in Los Prevenciones for many many many many many many many many many many many many many many many many many many many many many…"

and with that the tallest man slapped him on the back

"…years."

"I'm not whoever you just said."

The men in black suits wearing single eye patches laughed individually and collectively.

"Of course you are! As you can see by our records," and with that the smallest turned the terminal away from Alex, "there's only one Axel that works for RAW."

"And that's not me."

"Of course you aren't!"

And with that the smallest of the men turned and spoke to the tallest of the men's zipper. "Get everything ready."

A few of the men shuffled over to a plank of wood that looked like a teeter-totter stuck in the down position (or up position depending on which side you were looking at) and drug it to the center of the room. Another of the men began filling bottles with water, while a third tore a bath towel into rags.

"If you'll be so good as to lie down here," the smallest said.

"No," Alex answered, "I think I'll continue to be so bad as to lie up here."

"Hmmm, that puts a damper on the board of delight. Are you sure you won't let us sooth you into saying what we want you to say by tilting your head back, cramming your mouth with rags and pouring water onto them until you believe you're drowning."

"That doesn't sound delightful to me," Alex responded, "it sounds like torture."

"Of course it's not torture," the largest responded as he awoke, "It's merely our way of saying 'thank you' for lying to us."

"I'm not lying, at least I haven't started yet."

"See there you go, lying again."

"But if I said I was lying and then I wasn't lying wouldn't that mean I was a liar who wasn't lying?"

"You're trying to confuse us," said the largest man.

"Blanca."

He passed out again.

"Why does he faint when he hears the word 'Blanca'."

"Oh it's not the word Blanca," said the tallest of the men…

"It's the name Blanca," continued the shortest. "He's in love with a woman named Blanca on the fourth floor."

"Oh well that changes everything," Alex told him, "I'm looking for Blanca from the third floor."

And with those words everyone smiled and cheered and jumped up into the air.

"Third floor Blanca," said a man who was neither too tall nor short nor large nor small, "She's the nicest person we've ever met."

"Me too," said Alex, although he still didn't understand why his heart began to flutter.

After his heart had landed a man who appeared to be smaller than the smallest of the group said, "Won't you please lie on the board of delight now? We've got a few questions to ask you."

"Why don't you just ask me without the, um, delight."

"Because you might not tell us what we want to hear."

"Hear, hear," said the other men in the room.

"But why would you want me to tell you what you want to hear instead of the truth."

"Because then we're always right."

"Then how about I tell you what you want to hear right now and then you let me go and find Blanca."

There was some grumbling and finally an almost as tall as the tallest man said, "Will you come back afterwards and let us delight you?"

"As sure as I'm up here lying," said Alex.

"Okay, tell us what we want to hear."

"Um, you think it's a great idea to go back to watching people in the lunchroom and forget about me."

"Really? That's what we want to hear?"

"Absolutely."

"Great!" And with that all of the men turned so that their eye patches were facing him and chatted among themselves.

"One other thing," Alex asked.

"Who are you and how did you get in here?" asked one man.

"What do you want and how did you get in here?" asked another. Just then the largest man in the room awoke again and asked what was going on.

"We've forgotten about this guy but he just won't leave," said a man with a hook foot.

"He's looking for third floor Blanca," added the smallest.

"Oh really," stated the largest man and then he pointed upwards. "She was headed up there." It was then Alex noticed the ceiling was made of glass. And a great many people were staring down between their feet at them.

"I think I'll go now," Alex said. As he reached for the door handle a somewhat skinny man in a short legged moody blue suit and a tall haircut stepped out from behind a broom that was propped up next to the computer terminal.

"You won't find her through there."

"Through where?" asked a man wearing a patch over each eye.

"The back door," the somewhat skinny man whispered loud enough for everyone to hear. "The back door," he repeated just in case someone had missed it the first time.

"Why not?" asked Alex.

"Because we weren't, under any circumstance, going to allow her to sneak in through the back door."

"But she wasn't sneaking in."

"Hmmm, good point. Well we just couldn't have her leave through the back door."

"Why not?" asked Alex.

"You have a terrible habit of frequently repeating yourself at strange intervals," the somewhat skinny man said continuing, "A terrible habit etcetera." Just in case someone had missed it the first time.

"Why couldn't you let her leave through the back door?"

"Because we couldn't, what's so difficult to understand about that?"

Alex didn't understand so it was quite difficult.

"You see," the somewhat skinny man continued, "we were all standing right here, she came through and left and we didn't notice she'd been here until you pointed it out to us and if she went through that door then it means we'll never get the opportunity to see her come through the first time because she'll already be gone which means that while we were protecting the company from all manner of fiendish thingy (pronounced tingy) we were being infiltrated by random Blancas, not excluding the highly questionable one from the fourth floor. We can't have her go through the back door because it means we weren't doing our job and therefore, knowing that we always do our job…"

"…and extremely well, may I add…" added the smallest man.

"…she couldn't have gone through the back door."

"Okay," Alex answered, "which way did she go?"

"She was never here…"

Alex was perplexed again.

"…and when she left she went that a way."

"Away?"

"With that they all moved closer to the screen and stared intently."

STEPHEN WILDER

"Up the ladder."

It was then Alex noticed the ladder. It had been hard to see before because, being made out of glass, you could see right through it.

"Okay."

Alex walked to the base of the ladder and looked up. It went directly into the ceiling

"How am I supposed to get through up there?"

To a man the eye patch men laughed. And that man was the somewhat skinny man. "Are you a man, or what?" somewhat skinny asked him.

"Or what?" Alex asked.

"I could have guessed," said the smallest of the men.

"I could have guessed," said somewhat skinny in the event someone missed it.

Alex glanced upwards again and realized there was an opening although it was almost impossible to see because it was transparent as well. He thought it might be a little too small for him to fit through but at least he'd get the opportunity. He wondered if Blanca had the same opportunity. He looked up once more and then walked to the rear exit, opened the door, and stepped through.

"You're gonna regret that," shouted the largest man.

"He can't have done it," screamed the smallest man.

"You're right!" the others joined in.

"The woman's back in the lunch room," the man with a patch over each eye said gleefully. "She's obviously guilty of something."

As the door slammed shut Alex was quite happy to have put some distance between Alex and the men with patches. "Huh", Alex thought, "why has every thought referring to Alex gone into third-person." Alex sighed and considered everything that lay before Alex. A room filled from floor to ceiling with pieces of paper, boxes of paper, crates of paper, and surprisingly enough, big blue recycle bins.

"Hmm," Alex thought, "Where is Alex now?"

L

CHAPTER 5IVE:
ADVICE FROM
A
CATERWAULDO

Paper and more paper.

Stacked as high as trees in a redwood forest.

Alex had no idea where Alex was but didn't really care to know. Alex just wanted to get through this place as quickly as possible.

"I'll tell you where you aaare! It was a voice, of that Alex was certain, but the way it cut through the air made it sound more like a calico cat caught in the spokes of a moving Vincent Black Shadow. "You're in the Maaale Room."

"How do you know what Alex is thinking?" Alex asked.

"Well that's simple enough, aaall caterwauldos can read minds."

A pasty man in an ugly red & white knit cap with poofy ball on top and a nose so long, and pointed, it resembled a centipede leg, leaned over the ledge of one of the tallest stacks of paper. "Scruffy," Alex thought. And he was. Unshaven, unkempt and wearing a stained striped t-shirt, he seemed completely out of place or perfectly in place.

One.

Or the other.

Or both.

Or bother.

As the case may be.

The caterwauldo held an enormous upside-down mushroom-shaped glass pipe down towards Alex. Smoke billowed & bellowed from an opening at the top and Alex heard water sloshing back and fro inside it.

"You want to top this?" the caterwauldo asked.

"Uh, no thanks," Alex replied, "Alex is at work."

"Too baaad. Sure makes the day go by fstr! Or s l o   w   e   r. As the caaase may be."

"Is there some reason you whine like that?"

The caterwauldo lifted the opening to his mouth and flicked a flint. Bubbles danced and dazzled as the caterwauldo took an enormous mouthful of smoke. "Caterwauldo is aaa caterwauldo in a maaale room. You still got to aaask?"

Alex couldn't understand what the caterwauldo was saying through his enormous mouthful of smoke.

"Caterwauldo or caterwailer or marleywailer?" Alex asked politely only to be greeted with an exhaustive sigh. The caterwauldo leaned back and Alex heard the floom of bubbles. Soon enough a thick white smoke drifted down and the room smelled of burning rope.

"Is it a good idea to smoke with all this paper piled in here?"

The caterwauldo leaned over as his mouth fell open. More smoke drifted lazily upwards. "Whaaat else would you suggest!"

"That's the last question Alex asks," Alex thought else Alex would have to continue to listen to this noisy whiny mess of speech.

"Whaaat aaare you doing here aaanywho?" the caterwauldo shouted, "don't you know you aaare disturbing me?

"I was looking for a friend… Blanca."

"Blanca? She's not here. Caaan't Alex tell this is the maaale room?"

"Sorry, Alex is very sorry."

"Aaalex should be. You sure you don't waaant to hit this baaad boy?"

"How can Alex get out of here as soon as possible?" Alex thought.

"Easy," said the caterwauldo, "you just haaave to think of someone else."

"Think of someone else. What would that do?"

"Well it's a maaale room. That means you're thinking of yourself aaall the time. If you think aaabout someone else, you're obviously not maaale enough and you caaant staaay here. If you don't un'erstand here's a little ditty that will explaaain it succinctly."

With that the caterwauldo sang "me, me, me, I, I, I" and his voice dropped into baritone. It was surprisingly beautiful with its smoky flavor and mellow cherry blend. He opened his mouth, set in on a puffenhoof dance that consisted of flailing his arms and random scissor kicks, and sang…

I passed my face upon the stair,

tho it's neither here nor where

e'en tho I went both ways,

I recognized my frère

Exclaiming Holy Smokes!

Which he blew into my eyes

I thought we'd died and gone on home,

a long long then ago

Oh yes, we are,

those who puff the bowl

and now we are about to draw,

with the male who stoned the world

I gurzzled an' pumped his glasstly clong,

and made loose a snickery cough

I darzled with a covering hand,

he gave me a withering scoff

Unfazed he tripped

up the fazely stair

He left us all alone right there,

for a long, long time

And why? we knows…

he'd never loosed a cack

so now I sorely miss

the male who stoned the world!

As he completed the final line the caterwauldo froze and stared directly into Alex's eyes. After a good thirty seconds or so, as his arms began to slowly sag down to his side (they'd both been above his head when he stopped), he said, "W'dyaaa think?"

Alex didn't have a real answer… so he waited for help to arrive.

And

   he

      waited

         a

      long

           loooooooooooooong

                  loooooooooooooooong

                          time.

"So," Alex finally said, "can you tell Alex how to get out of here?"

With that the caterwauldo became highly agitated and screamed (a very manly scream complete with nostril puffs and hairy beary growls). "Get out of here… Go! Don't you know that this is the Male room? You're not allowed in here."

"Ah, I don't understand."

"Of course you don't. No self-respecting male would ask directions. He instinctively knows which beaver trail to tread. Be gone with you!"

Alex noticed that the caterwauldo was no longer speaking in his high-pitched, highly irritating, scree of sound and considered saying something about it to him. He was interrupted.

"You still here?"

"No," Alex answered.

"Good," was the response, "I don't think I could have stood another minute in your presence."

Alex drifted around to the other side of the mountain of paper and noticed it was smoldering. He didn't know if he should warn the caterwauldo lest he get caught up in another incomprehensible discussion that would eventually turn to sand grain universes, people with the ability to fly on kites like painted rats and hanging around the Jardin la Vie (complete with drum and organ solos).

"Um," Alex shouted up, "you're on fire down here."

The caterwauldo peeked over the other edge of spire of paper. His eyes were bleary and weary and red. "Hey," he said, "don't I know you?"

Alex didn't know how to answer. He really didn't know him per se but… "We met, ah, once before."

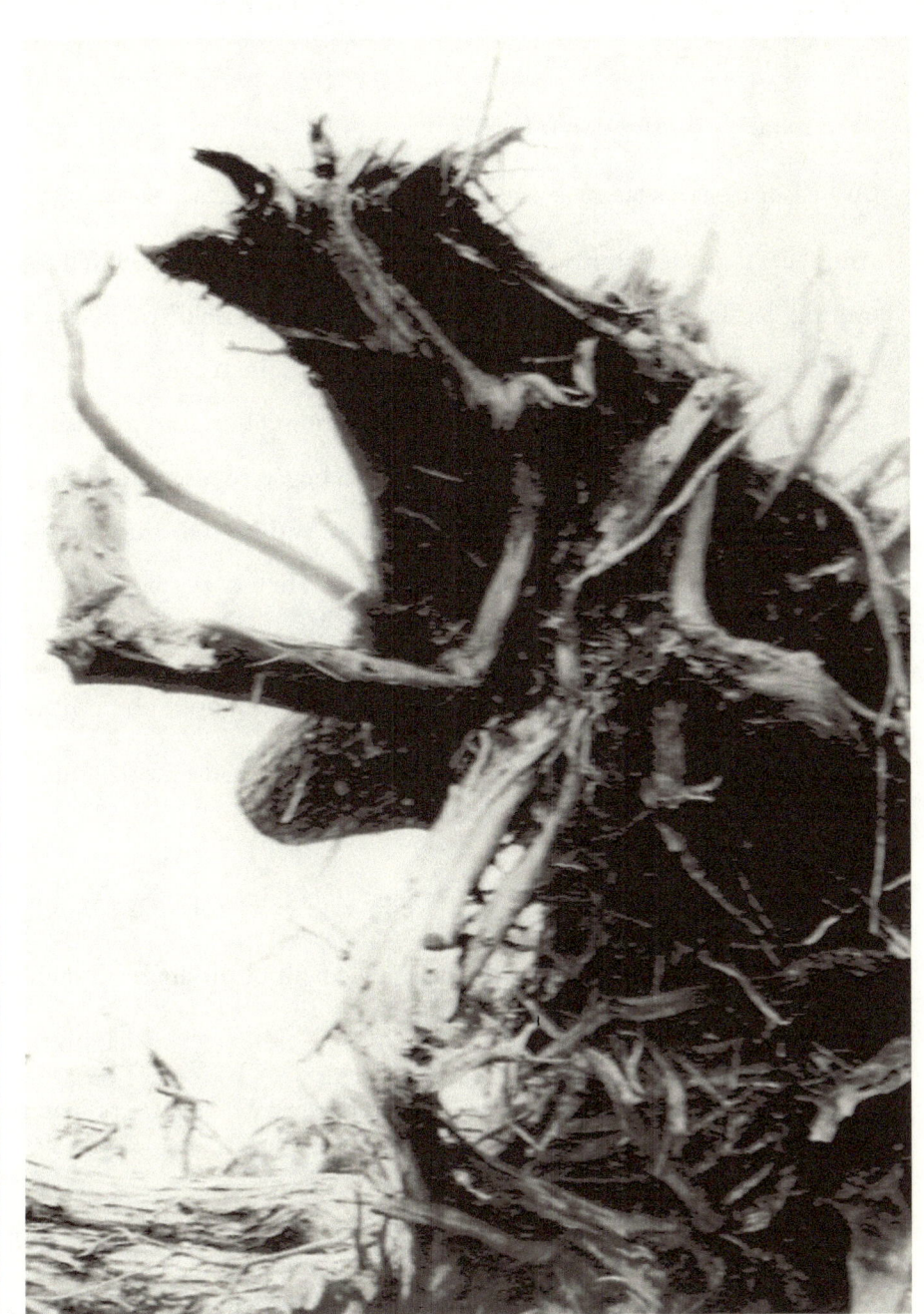

The caterwauldo held an enormous upside-down mushroom-shaped glass pipe down towards Alex.

RYAN SUFFERN

The caterwauldo held his mushroom-shaped blown glass kalian over the edge. "You want to top this?"

"Your stack's on fire down here."

"Whaaaaaaaaaaaaaaaaaaaaaaaaaaaaaaaaaaaaaaaaaaaaaaaaaaaaaaaat?"

And with that the caterwauldo dropped his pipe and it fell fell fell to the ground, landing at Alex's feet… crashing into a cracrickle of shards and splinters and sticklers. A woomphing poof of multicolored smoke streamed up into Alex's eyes and nostrils, sending him into a spasm of coughs, gasps, blinks and sneezes. His head began to alternately contract, expand, conspand and extract. He looked up and tried to find the caterwauldo but was greeted by empty space. He was perplexed, confused and dexelprep.

.thguoht eh "?aht tahW"

…sdrawkcab devom dna nwod dewols gnihtyrevE

.mih ot txen gnidnats won saw odluawretaC eht…

"!ojom dab yrev", dias eh ",ojom daB"

htaeneb esrevinu eht tuoba deksa dna ecaf sih ot pu dnah sih dleh xelA

.lianbmuht sih

srelknirps eht erofeb ereh fo tuo teg retteb eW" deilper odluawretaC

".ffo og

",yakO eb ll'tI"

.ffo tnew srelknirps ehT

"!gniniar s'tI" ,dias dna pu dekool, desucof xelA

Water streamed over them and the caterwauldo became extremely panicky...

    ...and then the intercom went off as well.

"Alex W. Bland please dial 7734... Alex W. Bland."

The caterwauldo sized him up. "That's you, huh?"

"Huh?" Alex answered.

"Later."

The caterwauldo was gone.

He left so quickly Alex was stunned. A red light flashed and a siren (which was obviously the caterwauldo recorded on a cheap cassette tape recorder) blared into the room. Alex wiped water from his eyes and staggered in a direction he considered to be forward.

A small mouse popped up from behind a stack of old accounting ledgers.

"Is the light that's flashing RED?"

"Huh? Yeah."

"Then we better get out of here."

The mouse turned and scampered away. Alex followed until he reached a door with a large silver handle. "Don't go in there," the mouse said...

    ...as Alex opened the door...

...".there's a cat in the kitchen."

L

CHAPTER 6IX:
PORKCHEFS
&
COOLCATS

CHAPTER 6IX

Alex was at the far end of a long long long long loooooooooooong industrial kitchen. Four times as long as the longest he'd ever seen. It was shiny silver and sparkling white and had the sterile primness you'd find behind the scenes at any hotel, mega-restaurant or 2001 space station.

Two very large men in white chef's hats and green gloop stained aprons were chatting only a few feet away from where he had entered.

"Excuse me," Alex said almost politely, "where's the nearest phone."

The two men ignored him and continued to chatter at each other without listening. The one on the right, a wild boar of a man who was large lengthwise and had an ugly pugly nose and five or six long huffenpoots of hair dangling from his chin, was obviously quite upset about something.

"How is it they choose that fool over me?" he asked the other man, a pot bellied bald headed fellow with eyes that bulged and ears that pointed towards the opposite side of his face.

"You forgot to hand in your menu."

"That's ridiculous," Pugly shouted, "I have it right here!"

And with that he jerked a piece of paper from his pocket and held it out to potbelly man. "See!"

Potbelly man ran his hand over his face, letting it linger over his mouth as if he wanted it to help him keep from saying something he'd regret.

"Well?" said Pugly.

"It may be a blessing in disguise," said Belly.

"What kind of disguise?"

"Huh?"

"Well if it's wearing a disguise I want to recognize it when it gets here. It deserves a butt whoopin'."

"That's not the point."

"What is the point then?"

"He's going to let you go and keep the other guy."

With that Pugly fell to the floor and began crying like a hungry newborn. "How can they do it to me," he shouted, "I've been working here for over 2 weeks!"

"Layoffs are bad for all parties concerned," said Belly, "Look at McTimmons in accounting, I hear he's going to get it and he's been with the company for close to 40 years."

"But he's just pork, they've got 100s of accountants!" Pugly screamed, "They've only got two executive sous-chefs and just one who specializes in cuisine from Madagascara!"

"That's true," said Belly, "but I wouldn't go spreading that around, there's already dark circles under everyone's eyes."

"Excuse me" Alex asked again.

Both men looked around as if they'd heard him but couldn't see him. Alex felt something brush against his arm but he was too busy waving to get the cooks attention to bother.

"I must be retained!" said Pugly.

"How long has it been since you were tained?" asked Belly.

"Way over three whole weeks give or take weekends and the few days I took off to watch the stranos return from Capiswallow!"

"The strano is a fine bird indeed! Plumage, like the eyelash, is important to this world."

And they raised imaginary glasses and clinked them.

"What are you going to do when you get your notice?" asked Belly.

"I'm not. I'm going to the meeting and have a word with them."

"Really? What are you going to say."

"Well, I've been debating between, NO and WRONG! What do you think?"

"Well wrong could apply to just about anything."

"That's good!"

"No, it's not."

"Not NO? So wrong is good."

"No wrong is not."

"I thought you said NO is NOT."

"No. I said no it's not"

"Right it is not."

"Right is not!"

"So Right is not and wrong is not so right is wrong!"

"That doesn't make sense."

"This makes sense though, right is wrong."

"NO! That's wrong."

"So I can say either one"

"Yes that is right."

"So yes is right, right is not, no it is not, so yes is no and right is wrong."

With that Belly slapped his forehead with an audible smack.

Someone leaned over to Alex's ear and said, "This has, like, been going on all morning. Dig it?"

Alex turned to find lithe and feline looking man in a porkpie hat and slick black suit standing next to him. He would have been startled but the man moved so fluidly, and the sound of his voice was so warm, it made him feel calm.

"Where'd you come from?" Alex asked.

"Oh I been here all along," the feline man said as he held out his hand and flashed a bright smile with one gold tooth, "my name's Chester." Alex felt for the button in his pocket, it was still there.

"Alex" and he held out his hand.

Then it's NOWHERE AT AT ALL!

GEORGE ADAMS

"Cool," Chester replied as he took Alex's hand and shook it lightly, "Nice ta meet ya Axel." As he said this he ripped a hipster smile that stretched from ear to ear and let Alex know he suddenly had a coolster jazzbo nickname. Alex hoped Los Prevenciones wasn't watching.

"Whatcha doin' listenin' to these two squares?"

"I'm looking for the nearest phone," Alex responded.

"Umm, that's a bad scene daddy. Only people looking for a phone today are the ones who aren't gonna be here tomorrow. Dig?"

"Sorry, but no."

"Let me try to put it to you another way." And Chester was gone. That he had disappeared so quickly was somewhat off putting to Alex. That he was now standing beside him again was extremely off putting. That Alex could now see completely through him, as if he was a ghost, put the off level up to gargantuan.

"If they call your name and you show up... gak!" Chester ran a finger across his throat.

"GAK!" Alex repeated. "I can't afford gak."

"Who can?" Chester said as his porkpie hat slowly floated upwards, away from his head. He reached up and snatched it back down.

"What should I do? Where should I go?"

Chester smiled and said, "Let me put it this way." And like a flash he was standing behind Alex.

When Alex turned he noticed that Chester was a little more transparent but his clothing had come back into full view. Perhaps it had something to do with his hat, which was now tied down to his head using white packaging string.

"Well," Chester said slowly and deliberately, "you're about as far down as you can be, so the only way is up."

"True."

"But the meeting is taking place up there." He pointed towards the ceiling. At least Alex thought he was pointing as the only thing visible was a raised black suit sleeve with a white shirt cuff sticking out. "And since the only way left to go is up, the logical conclusion is you'll end up at the meeting. Right?"

"What if I went some other way?"

"You know some other way other than up or down?"

"Sideways?" Alex asked this as a question or inquiry or something in between.

"Sideways, really? Where'll that get ya?" Before Alex could answer Chester was standing next to him again. "Nowhere man, really." Like a flash he was standing on the other side. "Now here is nowhere. See what I'm getting at? It's up or down or nowhere at all."

"But I don't want to go down and if I go up it'll be bad news."

"Well then I guess it's nowhere at all."

"But I don't want to stay here!" Alex felt flushed.

"Then it's NOWHERE AT ALL!" Chester said with a little extra inflection on the T ALL. "C'mon," he continued, "I'll show you."

And with that he took Alex by the shoulders (missing hands not withstanding) and spun him around and around until he was dizzy and staggering.

"I'm feeling a bit sick."

As Chester pushed Alex forward he said, "I got bit sick once... rabies I think they called it, bad news." And with that sad pronouncement they arrived at a door that said, 'NOWHERE AT ALL!' complete with exclamation. "Here you go," Chester said as the door opened (as if by magic), "keep a sharp eye and a dull wit... or is it sharp wit and a dull eye? Never can remember."

Alex felt himself pushed forward and he landed in a large smoke filled room. When the smoke parted slightly he could see three people were ("Are those people?" he thought) staring at him. He turned back towards Chester but all he could see was a glistening gold tooth.

"Later dude," was all he heard.

CHAPTER 7EVEN:
A CRAZY COFFEE BREAK

"Oh great, just great," said a man in a gaudy Red shirt with orange flowers all over it. He had an ink pen tucked behind his ear, which seemed a little incongruous considering the unused plastic protector in the pocket.

"Just ignore the idiot," said a tall and spindly man in a blue baseball cap standing next to him. The cap had a

YN

on the front and Alex wondered what team he supported.

"Maybe the dimwit will go away." YN quickly turned to face Alex and said, "What the hell do you want, can't you see we're having a coffee break?"

Alex started to answer but was interrupted by the third person, a tiny woman with large ears and wispy whiskers protruding from her upper lip and chin. "Would you like a…" She froze in mid sentence and slowly her eyes drifted shut.

"Oh great, just great," said the man in a gaudy shirt.

"Listen buddy we don't know what your game is but we're not buying any of it, are we Harry?"

"Not a solitary iota!" And with that gaudy shirt stepped forward and put out his hand. "Harry March, custodial services thirteenth floor and executive helipad!"

"I didn't know we had a thirteenth floor," Alex replied, "or a helipad. Not at all."

Harry's arm was left hanging in mid air as if someone would appear out of nowhere and shake it.

"Well there you go," said the tall man, "a-know-it-all."

"No a not-it-all," said Harry.

The woman slowly collapsed to the ground like a clump of balled up dirty laundry.

"Shouldn't we do something for her?" Alex asked.

"What would you suggest?" Harry said glancing over at the tall man.

"I don't know, help her over to a chair or something."

"Really Mister Smarty Ass," said the tall man, "which something would you suggest?"

Alex looked around the room. There were no chairs, only 4 four by six tables and a coffee machine on the one in the middle. The other tables had 7 coffee cups on each, so everything was perfectly balanced.

"Perhaps we could…" "Perhaps" answered tall man.

"Excuse me Matt," Harry interrupted, 'but I think you've got my coffee cup."

"Don't be an imbecile!" Matt, the tall Y N man, snarled back at him.

"No, I really think so." He held up his coffee cup. "See this one is from RAW Industries Multi-national. I think it's yours."

"All of the cups are from RAW. It's where we work."

"I beg to differ, we haven't worked in years."

"That may be true, but I've been drinking from this cup for the last three months."

"But wasn't my cup a little fuller than yours?"

And with that Harry held his cup out so Alex could see its dark black contents. It was about a quarter full but Alex didn't know what they were expecting him to say, so he answered, "Well um I don't..."

"Of course you don't," muttered the still sleeping Doris from the floor.

"Stop stressing out and wake up!" commanded Matt.

"Anyway," Harry continued, "If you compared our cups... his would be fuller than mine."

"Don't be ridiculous," shouted Matt as he held his cup out for Alex to see. Sure enough it was filled nearly to the top.

"I think..."

"When the hell did you start that obnoxious habit," Matt screamed at the top of his lungs. With that he handed his RAW cup to Harry who in turn reciprocated the action.

"Would you care for a cup o' Java?" asked Harry.

Alex figured his expected answer had gotten him in good with the man in the Hawaiian shirt and now he'd be able to be on his way... wherever that was. "I don't..."

"And you never will," said the still sleeping Doris.

"Sweet God you idiot," Matt shouted, "are you sure we have enough?"

Harry took one of the cups from the table furthest to the right and handed it to Alex. "Of course we do." He picked up a silver industrial pot (Where'd that come from?) and slowly poured a stream of fine dirt into the cup. "There you go."

Alex didn't move. He merely stared into his cup.

"What in hell are you doing here?" shouted Matt as he took off his cap and wiped his bald pate.

"I'm looking for Blanca..."

"Fourth floor or thirteenth floor?"

"I didn't know there was a thirteenth floor."

"You see! There you go again," Matt shouted, "spreading terrible lies about the thirteenth floor and everyone on it."

"Not at all, it's just..."

"It's no such thing," snoozed Doris.

"You know there's a fourteenth floor, don't you?"

"Yes," Alex answered.

"Well how in hell could we have a fourteenth floor without a thirteenth? What are you, daft?"

"No..."

"A messy hand was the price he'd have to pay to get away from Matt, Harry and Doris"

CHRIS BROWNING

"What do you think, it's just hovering up there waiting for the right moment when it can fall and crush the people on the 12th floor?"

"That's ridiculous."

"It's your hypothesis," Matt screamed, "not mine!"

"You know what else is ridiculous?" Harry said emphasizing the what. "This riddle... how is bitter day old pie like a sailor who's been at sea for 20 years? Do you know what the answer is?" Both Alex and Matt shook their heads.

"Then what good are either of you!" Harry walked away from them, stepping over Doris, and made his way to the corner and sulked.

This wasn't one of your ordinary run-of-the-castle sulks either! It was like a dictionary for the sulking community: a foot stompin', beside himself grumblin', complainin' out loud, dirty look dishing, enraged gesturing, frowny faced

And before the typing of the sulking sentence was complete, WHAM a kite drifted through the room, its odd tale

d r a g g i n g

behind it.

"It's sad for sure" the small grey rat said in a disheartened voice, "I was minding my own business, enjoying the muted tones and rustic feeling of my own portrait when I head someone or something say, psssst... hey... you. Well I didn't know which of the five W's to think! I mean I could hear the voice right in my ear but I couldn't see a thing. Could you, it asked, help me find my way to the thirteenth floor? Who was it? What was I supposed to do? When did it want to leave? Why ask me? At first I thought it might be the big cheese, you know, the pouch rat in the clouds, but then it dawned on me that the voice didn't even know there's no thirteenth floor in this building."

"Why are we listening to this dirty rat?" Matt shouted as he sniffed the air. Harry grumbled something from the corner and the rat turned to him and said, "Shouldn't you be wearing a shirt instead of a bunch of flowers?"

"Oh great," Harry answered, "just great."

"Anyway," the Rat continued, "I was hoping that something strangurious, wondrous and mysterious would happen at just the right moment.

And something did.

A man in a business suit appeared out of nowhere, shook Harry's hand and said "Gladaknowya" before disappearing just as quickly.

"Forget it' said the Rat, 'if we can't keep people from the thirteenth chapter from showing up I don't have to tell a story that no one wants to hear anywhere. And with that the Rat tugged on the tale of the kite and drifted away.

"I didn't know there was a thirteenth chapter," Alex said as the Rat floated away waving a clenched fist at him.

"Holy Children of the Pope!" Matt raged, "There isn't one!"

"No one? Then how'd this book start?" said the snoozing Doris.

"With a forward," Matt said snappily.

"Wouldn't that make the twelfth chapter the thirteenth?" asked Harry.

"Not without one," Doris snored.

"Should we get him back?" Alex asked.

"No. Better to get him front because it's easier to understand what someone's rambling on about," Harry said knowingly.

"That's stupid, stupid, stupid," Matt added and then he stopped before adding another stupid. "Him front was no better than him back!"

"That's an odd thing to say," Alex stated.

"No… stupid… that's an odd thing to say."

Doris' eyes snapped open and she slowly rose to her feet. "Coffee Break," she shouted as she pulled a small silver hammer from God knows where. Crash. Tinkle. Crinkle. Trash.

She smacked each of their coffee cups until only handles remained. The Java burst into the air like powder from a puff. She sighed, muttered something about snow in heaven, returned the hammer to God knows where and drifted back to her comfy spot on the floor.

"Well where did the time go?" Alex asked as he looked down at his watch and backed away from the three.

"That explains it," shouted Matt.

"Time is gone," Harry said gleefully.

"I guess space is next," the re-snoozing Doris mumbled quizzically.

"It's just a saying," Alex added showing them his watch, "it's 10:01."

"WRONG!" Harry puffed, sticking his arm out. "It's 12:21 exactly." Sure enough his watch read 12:21. The casing was cracked and the face smashed but you could still read the numbers.

"He's right you know," Matt added holding out his arm. His watch said it was three twelve. It was also smashed.

"I'm pretty sure it's ten oh two."

"But you just said it was ten oh one."

"Yeah, but…"

"Well now you're saying it's ten oh two, make up your mind."

"I'm sure it's almost exactly correct." Alex added.

"Almost? That means it's never right."

"Um."

"My watch is at least twice as accurate as yours."

"Mine… two!"

Doris sleepily held up an hourglass and said, "Never fails!"

"I've got to get back to looking for Blanca." But no one was listening to him.

Matt dropped to his knees and turned the hourglass over and over and over again to watch the grains of sand tumble through the narrow center.

Harry pretended to ignore him but kept checking his watch against the hourglass and mumbling something about pine coffee.

Alex backed all the way up against a wall and felt something jab him in the back. He turned to find a white doorknob dripping red paint. He wasn't certain he wanted to touch it but he eventually decided a messy hand was the price he'd have to pay to get away from Matt, Harry and Doris (who, it seemed, suddenly realized how much they hated each

She smacked each of their coffee cups until only handles remained.

CHRIS BROWNING

other's company and began hitting each other with new cups o' Java) so he carefully and slowly turned the knob and peeked in.

It was a beautiful garden.

And it looked better than nowhere.

O

CHAPTER 8IGHT:
A PRINCESS &
A GARDEN OF BANG

Garden?

Well it wasn't a garden exactly, but it sure looked like one.

At first glance Alex was fooled by the exotic looking collection of plants, flowers and growth which had been crammed Willy & Nilly into a multitudinous multicolored mass but soon it was easy for him to see that everything about this garden was artificial.

The tip off might have been the vast arrangement of Nongke and One-Beef Orchids or abundance of No Se Green Peppers but actually it was because he could see two guys in grey jumpsuits (the aforementioned Willy & Nilly) pulling false flora out of huge cardboard boxes and sticking, pasting, jamming and forcing it into anything they could reach.

Into the imported dirt (which appeared to be Javanese) covering the floor beneath them.

Onto large formations of masking tape & viscous vellum which was molded into bogus trees, vines, vrees and tines.

Unto a perfidious plot of pipe cleaners, paper-mâché and pliable piles of putty that spelled out 'WELCOM'. It was obvious neither Willy nor Nilly spent much time in skool.

But something else made it clearly apparent to Alex that this wasn't a living garden far beneath the ground in the depths of a huge corporate plant.

Sure there was a beautiful baby bunting blue sky.

And fabulously fluffy white clouds.

And a sun that was a ball of golden yellow joy.

And they were all painted in one of the most un-artistic (or least artistic) manners he could recall.

Well perhaps not the most (or least), because he could still picture the childish work of the painter with the toothbrush moustache… a reflection which spilled over onto his own third grade art (including the famous turkey-made-out-of-a-hand-print that won him acclaim at the dinner table), before his thoughts dripped into a Rorschach like pattern that was formed by the scrambled eggs he'd spilled last Sunday (a truly terrible morning when his RAW oeuvre was surprisingly unesculent and his take home work wouldn't become catch up). No, this may not have been the worst he'd seen, but it was fairly close.

It was second grade art, for certain.

The two men worked frantically as he watched… and if they knew he was there they didn't do anything to acknowledge his presence. Willy was very high strung and Nilly seemed on the verge of breaking from tension.

"What'll we do," Nilly asked? His reedy voice began at a cat-song screech before ascending into the trembling glissando of an orchestra of detuned ukuleles.

"Keep working," Willy screamed frantically, "she's almost here! She's almost here!!" The tenor of his baritone betrayed that he knew it to be an otiose task. As Alex listened to the bits and baggles of chatter their story became clear.

Willy & Nilly had been tasked with preparing a lovely and hopefully relaxing space for a RAW executive who'd been asked to ponder the true meaning of existence (which meant getting the most out of the underachieving 'RAW Overachiever's Club').

They instantly set about preparing the space by painting an entire room (the one we're currently in) black and then filling the ceiling, walls and floors with an exact replica of our universe (there are 11 you know!) from the tumescent P.O.V. of the big bang at conception. It was stunning in its arrangement, beautiful in its execution and may have been acceptable except for two elements (or lack thereof):

First, in order to achieve a verisimilitude of accuracy, they pumped all of the oxygen out of the room... this did NOT go over well when their immediate supervisors and a quality control team entered to evaluate the neatness & craftsmanship of the beginnings of existence. It did bring about the singular axiom "all supervisors should consider travelling in their own craftsman ship when entering a vacuum" though.

Second, the supervisors who replaced the previous supervisors were, more than anything else, afraid of being fired. Oh they were exquisitely happy with Willy & Nilly's rendition but were un-exquisitely unhappy with the theme because Executive Viper Residents of Budgeting And Development, as a whole, were universally anti-apportion and pro-growth. This static position would make most people's hair stand on end (including Alex) and would invariably interfere with the company's ability to conduct business, but it's always said there's no telling with executives and that goes double for the Executive Viper Resident, a position held by few and wanted by fewer.

Yes, neither Nilly nor Willy had bothered to ask who'd been given the job and since both had known Manny Fewer for quite awhile they figured it was his for the giving. They reasoned that a cosmic representation of the contracting and expanding beginning of both matter and thought was just what was needed to make him happy and allow them to keep their jobs for a fixed number of years. They wanted it to be perfect because they thought it a matter of principle (but not the principle of the matter).

How wrong.

It wasn't until they were putting on the final touches (post vacuum visit but pre replacement supervisors) that they were informed outright that someone from outside RAW had been selected by the executive search committee.

The committee had looked far and low and found Princess Wanout... who'd instantly became the leading candidate on a list of one.

They knew she would put things right and RAW's days of dismal complacency would be left behind.

And things needed to be ultra right! At least that's what RAW's executives told themselves as they worried about this dubious fact and that unseemly circumstance and these unsolvable problems and those uninteresting things.

They also knew Princess Wanout (who hated space and the idea of the universe's contracting/expanding birth even more than the girlish name her parents had bestowed upon her) would want a garden. A place where a Viper Resident could ultimately relax and ignore the big RAW questions, only taking into consideration what needed to be considered. Where she'd never need care about the realities of a harsh world.

She didn't want a bogus bang of bigness.

She wanted plenary paradise for platitudes.

And they did too.

So Nilly and Willy had exactly 23 hours, 56 minutes and 50 seconds to fix the situation.

And now it was 23 hours, 56 minutes and 48 seconds later and Alex was listening to the two men chatter like mice.

"What in helf-all-mighty is going on here!"

A deafening voice blasted their inner ears like a cymbal crash. Drums pounded a message across their malleus to their brains and they knew the time, like Prince (which is what her friend called her), was nigh.

"You are fired. You are fired. You are fired and YOU are fired."

She had a face like a puffy pig eating pastries and was wearing clothes that made her look like the head of a cheerleading school or a Sloppy Joe.

"But there're only three of us here," Willy protested, "I think you might have been looking in the mirror we had previously used to reflect light in a stirring tribute to the Planck Epoch."

"Or Planck error as those of us who believe the universe is half empty like to say."

Prince screwed up her face like she was putting on lipstick.

"I mean the mirror we are using to represent the light that is brighter than the sun in this wonderful garden," Willy said trying to change the subject.

"Since I never second guess myself and I never change my mind I guess that mirror means I'm fired." Prince said "But before I go I think I'd better hire the most qualified person available to be my assistant."

"Manny Fewer?" Willy asked.

"No… me!" She said forcefully. "And I guess that upon my leaving I'll have to be promoted to EVRBAD, 'cause I wouldn't want the company to go too long without someone to ponder the big non-questions. But then I think I will rehire ME and after I pass a security check I'll be cleared to come back to work! And in line for two paychecks! Maybe I'll even get a massive payout from the lawsuit I'm going to file against me for unlawful termination."

She considered this final budget busting datum for a split second (which seemed like an eternity to Nilly who was measuring it in Planck time) and said, "Heckfire, I'm worth it!"

It was then she noticed Alex standing across from her and asked, "Have I fired you yet?"

"Appears so, 'though they seem to have disagreed with you."

Which was partially true since neither Willy nor Nilly knew Alex was there until the next paragraph.

With that Prince looked to both Willy & Nilly who, although surprised to see Alex standing there, turned away quickly and began stuffing more and more false flowers and such into any empty space they came across… of which there was a lot. The Such weren't nearly as non-fragrant as non-flowers but added to the lot's overall non-effectiveness due to a lengthy manufacturing process which included the mundane and time consuming practice of rolling each individual Such in a pile of moose dung and crushed lilac.

"Well I guess I'm gonna have to re-hire you boys and then let you go!"

Both of them smiled, said "Thanks" and broke down in tears.

"You're welcom!" It seemed she hadn't spent much time in skool either.

With that she turned to Alex and said, "Now what am I gonna do with you?"

"It depends," Alex answered, "If I AM already fired there's nothing you can do because I don't work for you and if I'm not fired then you must have changed your mind which we know you never do and I'll just continue on my way."

"That sounds logical. I'm not sure I like it. What do you think?"

Alex started to answer but realized she wasn't talking to him. She'd turned and began shouting in her deafening snicker skree tone, thereby revealing that someone was standing behind her.

Now, she wasn't exactly large (other than her piggy head) so it was clearly within reason that someone was either the thinnest man in the world or a person so nondescript, so anti-spectacular, so so, that it was hard to notice he was there.

The man answered. But neither Prince nor Alex paid attention.

"You're fired then," Prince said to Alex.

"Sorry, but I don't work for you. Remember if you fire me it means you've already fired me so you can't… and you can't."

"Um yes."

"We really haven't settled the issue," Alex told her, "so I guess I'm kind of in limbo."

"Hmmm, not bad." A voice came out of nowhere.

Both Alex and Prince looked towards the man who was anti-spectacular but he appeared to be either picking his nose or pulling lint from his sweater.

They didn't really care which.

"Not as hep as some of my better leaps of logic, Alex, but it'll do." It was Chester, either half way between fading in and out or halfway between fading out and in.

"You are so fired," Prince screamed at him. The veins in her pink neck were bulging, the bun on her Sloppy Joe head unbraiding, the stick on her puffy lips smudging.

"Fat chance," Chester replied.

Now she was almost apoplectic. Fury raced around behind her eyes causing them to twitch, and twitter, like a hungry baby bird's.

"You are fired fired!"

"You can't fire me lady, 'cause I don't work for you," Chester said.

"That's my bit," said Alex.

"As a matter of fact," Chester continued, "I don't work for RAW. Work's not my thing." Chester pronounced it thang.

"Oh that's new," said Alex.

The notion of someone not working for RAW had never crossed her mind. And it had never zig-zagged in her mind nor circumsnakulated through her mind either. "Then what are you doing here?" she questioned.

Alex was wondering the same thing, but not as harshly.

"I'm a consultant."

"Consultant?" She turned to anti-spectacular man and repeated herself, "You are fired fired!"

Alex didn't hear anti-spectacular's response because he'd already turned his attention back to Chester and asked, "Do you think I could be a consultant?"

"You show promise!" Chester smiled widely.

Anti-specs response (which we've heard, second-hand of course, began like this... "Fired? I-" No one was paying attention after that) barely made a dent in Prince's next almost thought which came out as, "What in the world could you ever consult about?"

"A whole universe of things," Chester responded. "Contractually I'm paid twice as much as the highest paid low level executive on the payroll with greater than five years experience (as long as they don't work half of the maximum number of minimum overtimes (under certain conditions)) and an equal number of degrees, Kelvin or Centigrade."

"???" Prince looked confused and Alex didn't know if it was because she didn't understand the degree to which these things helped his consulting or if she was trying to figure out how Chester had gotten a better employment contract than she did.

Alex figured it was the perfect time for it so he handed her his jar of mayonnaise. One of her top teeth (which looked like the incisor of a sibling vole) extended over her bottom lip in a sort of smile. She was stunned into a second's silence.

Chester sighed. "I help department S50 determine the internals necessary to understand the external pressure being exerted upon the work force by X factors as indicated by my formula for success UR2X=2C.

"X?" Prince shouted, ignoring her one second of peace, "That's stupid!"

"Exactly!" Chester said smiling even wider.

"Cool," Alex added, thoroughly impressed because he was able to solve the equation before Prince.

"Cool," said Willy.

"Cool," said Nilly.

Prince was unhappy with their chilly reception to Chester's obvious insubordination.

"You need to tell me what you mean," she said fiercely.

With that Chester began to disappear slowly. "I'm never mean," he said, "I'm always even. Long gone daddies, hate to leave you with this yee-ya."

"Uncool," said Alex.

"Uncool," said Willy.

"Unto a perfidious plot of pipe cleaners, paper-mâché and pliable
piles of putty that spelled out 'WELCOM'."

THOMAS MOORE

"Very uncool," said Nilly.

Prince turned bright red and it was easy to see that her inner dialogue was becoming steam heated.

"Don't you leave," she said, "Tell me what you're saying!"

Chester was now merely a gold tooth smile and a hat and Alex figured he wouldn't be coming back. Consultants always disappear when you need them.

"You," she said to Alex, "You're coming with me to explain what's going on down here!"

"But I don't know what's going on down here." Alex wasn't lying. He didn't. He knew what WENT on down here, but he didn't know what WAS going on. Except maybe for the bit about Chester but then again that was what went on and not what was going on now. "And I gave you a jar of mayonnaise."

She turned her attention. "Then what about you two?"

Willy & Nilly didn't know how to respond. They remained quiet.

"Playing hard to get?" she snapped. "Then I'll just have to hire the both of you and give you promotions."

"But we've both already maxed out to the Peter!" Willy answered.

"What would that mean to RAW's standard operations?" Nilly asked.

"Never mean," a disembodied voice said to no one.

"What would it do to the universal constant? How could I unexpect the unexpected if the plan is interrupted by another promotion?" Willy entreated.

Prince's answer was just about to make its way past her puffy lips but she was interrupted by a very surprised Nilly. "Hey isn't that 3rd floor Blanca?"

As one they looked over and, sure enough, there she was quietly creeping through the non-garden. She held her nose as she opened a door covered in non-flowers, no vines, and faux flora.

"Blanca, esoy s devpmf," Alex shouted, but she didn't understand. As he spoke his words had slipped one space to the right on the keyboard and turned into a jumbled mess.

"No use shouting after her," Willy said, "she's in love with some guy named Alex."

Alex's brain made a decision right then and there to eventually tell him its big secret but everyone was distracted by…

"I DON'T CARE IF YOU DON'T WANT TO PAY ATTENTION TO ME I'VE GOT SOMETHING TO SAY!"

They each turned to find anti-spectacular man huffing and puffing, gasping and groaning, inhaling slowly and exhaling quickly.

"I think I'm having a heart attack," He added.

They raced to him, realizing he wasn't quite as unspectacular as they thought.

But Willy began to pant and huff as well.

As Nilly clutched his chest and took a soft gasping breath.

Prince tugged at her sweater and shook her jar of mayo at them. "What's wrong with you idiots?"

"I think," Alex said, "that all of the air is being sucked out of the room."

And Alex left.

Right away.

CHAPTER 9INE:
THE FAUXNIMAL'S TALE

CHAPTER 9INE

Alex was amazed at how quiet it was behind him down the allway. It was an allway because it was a corridor that went off in all ways at once but led to the same place… which was where ever the opposite of where he was is. It seemed everyone knew the non-garden was something close to avoid.

"Hey Kid! It's great not to see you again!" Alex looked over to see a wild boar of a man who was large lengthwise and had an ugly pugly nose and five or six long huffenpoots of hair dangling from his chin.

The man smiled widely.

Alex frowned and scratched his head and brushed his cheek and massaged his temples and rubbed his eyes and picked his nose and itched his philtrum and— Oh! Now he recalled where he'd seen him before.

Pugly the Chef took Alex by the arm and shoved a small flaky pastry into his mouth as he led him away from the non-garden. Alex chewed and chewed and chewed and chewed and chewed and chewed and chewed and chewed and chewed and… it wouldn't go down.

"Yum Yum Yum!" Pugly shouted with delight echoing in his voice. "I know how much you love Venus's-ears wrapped in water dough!"

Since Alex had never eaten such a bizarre thing before he responded, "My mownt mow mhat miss miz!"

"But you just did!" Pugly said of the former without stopping to consider the ramifications of knowing what had been written and "Don't talk with your mouthful" he said climbing to the latter.

Alex spit the un-appetizer onto the floor of the allway with a ptffftp. "Sorry, it was just awful."

"Odd, I thought it just wonderful." Pugly pondered this for a second before he added, "I guess it evens out! I'm full of wonder, you're full of awe and it seems just enough."

Alex looked at him quizzically and sorted through a multiple guess of things that lined up in his thoughts.

A lot needs to be considered here.

Be steady.

See what he wants.

Delight shouldn't really echo in a voice.

Even in a story such as this.

Effort will help me get through this chapter.

Gee why am I doing this?

As Alex leafed through all of the above Pugly said delightfully, "My my my, that's a lovely non-flower in your pocket. How did you come by it?"

Alex patted himself down like a cop until... a plastic orchid? After considering how it'd got there he said, "I came by it as I left that non-garden." He handed it over to Pugly who sniffed its underside delicately.

"Odd," Pugly said. "It smells even worse than I recall which isn't bad because I've never smelled one before kid."

Alex was fairly certain he'd never non-smelled a Nongke either. Pugly shouted, "Delightful! Wonderful! Awful! Where can I get another one?"

"They're still in there." And with that Alex pointed back towards the non-garden of less than somethingness (with a silent vacuum).

Pugly considered Alex's reply for a third or so and said, "Maybe it's not so great I haven't met you again!" He considered his own words for a sixth and added, "All this talk of non-gardens and Nongkes... you tend to communicate in riddles and rhymes and rages and rogets! I'm not sure I dig you a bit... and I know I don't like pretending or postending non-gardens!"

"You ever heard the saying, Be careful if you pretend to be a bee because you are what you pretend to be a bee?"

"I said it seven times in the past five minutes," Pugly responded, "how many times have you said it?"

Alex began to count.

"Wow! You are so fired."

Both Alex and Pugly were nearly frightened out of their shoes but it was Pugly who fell to the ground sobbing sockless like a turtle. Princess Wanout was blocking their egress. Alex turned back and looked towards the non-garden. The vacuum was still silent but nothing had changed.

"Weren't you...," Alex asked.

"And I always have been."

Pugly glanced up towards her scowl. It was one of the new super deluxe flat bottomed models and it frightened him even more.

"I see you there," she said in a stern voice, "and I see you here too!"

Pugly moaned and cried and shivered and shuddered and... her scowl was enormous and carried a lot of weight.

"Why don't you go, relax and take a load off? I hear it's very quiet in there."

With that Pugly looked over at the non-garden and began blubbering garbage like a hunted whale. He was scowling now.

"Go on," she said, "This one and I have some business."

Pugly drifted past her snittering, "It turned out not to be nice not meeting you again. Come by if you want some Bau Yu and Black Fungus pastry pie!"

Just the thought made Alex's stomach turnover and now he felt like he was standing on his head. He attempted to smile but frowned instead. The whole world seemed to be going tipsy-piggledy.

"I've heard a stern rumor you're following blankets and headed to the 13th floor?" She said, her scowl having sailed on to be replaced by an open grin.

"I have no idea what you mean by blankets... and there's no 13th floor."

"Have faith."

"In something which doesn't exist?"

"What do whiches have to do with anything other than Halloween? And tell me Mister Smarty, if you don't believe a place exists how do you ever expect to arrive?"

"That's the point!"

"I need you to take something there for me so maybe it's just a matter of you having someone explain to you how to get there."

"Someone can tell me someway to get to somewhere that doesn't exist? Who?"

"Fauxnimal of course!"

"Fauxnimal?"

"Of course!"

"Who's that?"

She quickly turned and looked around shouting, "Where?"

"Fauxnimal?"

She looked around again, "Where?"

"I gotta go." Alex had grown oh so tired of her nonsense.

"Roger!"

"Oh Kay, I'll play along... over and out!"

Alex walked away from her and the non-garden.

"Roger Fauxnimal! One of the six or seventy-three greatest minds in busy-ness. The saying goes that you don't know busy-ness until you've been Roger'd!"

"How..."

"Good question! Well the Faux, that's what his friend calls him, doesn't get in your face and tell you what to think, he likes to sneak up and…"

"But…"

"Stop skipping ahead! Anyway he's an expert at taking information from a million different sources and massaging it into exactly what he thinks you need to hear and doing it at an incredible rate of speed! So quickly that you don't have time to believe a word he says! He puts the ness in busy. For example, have you heard the saying "No Shes, No Sice, No Shit, Rover!""

"Uh, no"

"It was him done it all! Those shes don't know what to do about his onslaught of thinks, syllables, looks and hears."

"I can't imagine why."

"Everyone is completely unexcited about them!"

"Hard to believe."

"Well Roger can make you believe better than anybody."

"Not counting you of course. I bet you believe better than all of us put together."

"One time he told a story about a boy who was cryin' 'til a wolf came by and raised him up. Nobody could call him anything but truthful because no one had heard something somewhat similar. Without the slashing blade of truth he had convinced…"

"Con knived?"

"…them the miracle of the flying monkeys wasn't just a fairytale…"

"…but…"

"Will you please stop skipping forward!?!"

Alex didn't know how to answer a rhetorical question but considered the various possibilities.

A wango crooshy voice sounding like a blender full of marbles drifted from behind them and disturbed their discourse.

"This sounds like 'n interestingly boring conversation!"

"Rupert, Rupert Griffin you old sea dog!"

Prince obviously knew the grey skinned old man who'd silently glided up beside them.

"Good to see you 'gain my lil barrier cutie!"

Alex didn't like the look of him. Or the sound of him. Or anything about him.

"Whooze yer friend?" he asked Prince, casting an evil eye towards Alex. And evil it was. Just like the one on the other side of his head. They moved about in opposite directions, never stopping for a second, just like him. His pacing, moving forward, dropping back, swinging from side to side and constant chatter made Alex feel a little seasick.

"Alex W. Bland, he's gonna take something up to the 13th floor for me."

"The Fingertips (Pt.2) guy? Doeszee know the words?"

"Fauxnimal'll tell him everything he kneads to dough."

With that Griffin tilted one eye towards him and began to recite in a high pitched air raid whine…

Nuttin' Hugh can cook can be underdone

Nuttin' Hugh can fling can be unflung

Nuttin' Hugh can flee without catching some

But he's mostly flea free!

Griffin began a dance that in past times would have been called a tarantella but in modern times is referred to as the Colombian Boogaloo. Prince began to move her shoulders up and down and then slapped her knee in time to Griffin's foot movements while singing "I love his whiffenpoofs!" ad nauseum until Alex began to feel ill.

"Who's Hugh?" Alex screamed but didn't get a response.

The two dancers drifted back and forth across the hallway as though they were in the power of a full moon and spinning earth. They turned slowly... slowl...

"Excuse me," Alex said, "I'm going to keep heading, um, this way. Catch up with you later." He slowly backed away as they began to whoop and holler and shoop de shoop.

Alex turned, wiped his brow and smiled at how lucky he was to get away from Prince without being pseudo-fired.

"She's never really fired anyone."

Alex was stunned to find Griffin drifting up along side him. He looked back and Prince was still doing her version of the Colombian Boogaloo.

"Alex looked over to see a wild boar of a man…"

HELEN E. SCHROEDER

"She won't notice we're gone for another twenty or ten minutes. She's like that." Griffin continued to slowly drift behind Alex, which made him very uncomfortable. He tried to keep moving forward while keeping one eye on Griffin, which was a very hard thing to do. Periodically he banged into and/or bounced off of one allway wall or the other.

After a few minutes of silently following Alex, Griffin declared "Well we're here!"

"Yes we are!" said a strange looking man with teary eyes, dripping jowl cheeks and a huge slot of hair missing from the back of his head. "We are here!"

Alex said, "You must be Roger Fauxnimal."

"That would be accurate under most circumstances including this one but I have something I feel I must add to this important albeit perhaps consequential, perhaps not, but highly devastating piece of information which I've picked up from a source (whom I believe wants to remain nameless or perhaps be renamed maneless like me) who upon very good authority and a little prying and prodding of a sort we don't usually like to talk about in mixed company, which I noticed isn't mixed at the moment but could be if we wait a few hours or so. Got it?"

"I'm uh looking for someone, Blanca maybe you know—"

"Then you want to go to the 13th floor! I'm just the one to get you there if you really want to go... I say that because it's not really a place most people can get to, well not really, it's a place most people can get to, it's really not a place that's not a place to get to, if you get my meaning!"

"I don't," Alex answered.

"Then I'll have to explain it all to you."

Alex sighed and sat down. He suddenly wondered if love was all it's cracked up to be… but he still didn't understand why he was thinking such a thing.

Which oddly enough, sounded like 'ting' when he thought it.

A

CHAPTER 10N:
FAUXNIMAL'S BOOGALOO

Roger Fauxnimal began to sway to and fro. His mouth was open wide (displaying a set of teeth where each seemed to have its own agenda... "We make a motion that we attempt to smile" said the mandibles in a show of unity, but they were overruled by the angry maxillas, biting back hard) and his brow furrowed. Tooth and frown. He stripped down to a sheer black stretch tight skin suit and broke into an interpretive dance the likes of which had never before been seen. He sang in a cold, clear voice.

Down the dark deserted allway
Past the upwards downstairs
There's a small coat closet
It's better not to stop there
'Cuz you'll start to feel dizzy
Don't watch the phloomping red light
If you're ultra heavy or way too slim
You'd better turn to the right!

Upon the 'singing' of this last line it dawned upon Alex that Fauxnimal was not dancing, per se, but acting out the steps that would need to be followed for him to make his way to the non-existent 13th floor (with just an smidge of the Colombian Boogaloo thrown in for good measure). Griffin had joined in with a kind of shadow dance, always a Planck millisecond behind but mimicking Fauxnimal's spins, flips, gyros and spyros with the precision of a drunken sailor in a tin roof out-house. Fauxnimal quickly broke into a high-step march and sang like an alter boy with smoker's lung.

Then you spit at the door way

And ring the shing-a-ling bell

Take the key down off of the 2nd shelf

For room eleven or twenty one twelve

Insert said key and shake the handle

'Til it opens half the way

Crawl face first down the corridor

You're on your way happy daze

At this point Griffin sang along in a voice even a mother would smother. He drifted in and out of a kind of tortured harmony that was a semi-quiver above a fifth and a demi-hemi-quaver below being sharp.

You're on the way to making a 13th floor plan

It's really there!

It's truly somewhere! (sang Griffin)

If you actually care!

It may be up or down no one knows where the 13th floor can

Be is it over here? (sang Griffin)

Where's not exactly clear?!?

Fauxnimal fell to his knees and sang & cried as though he'd just finished shooting his favorite dog (again). It was a highly emotional performance and for a second Alex considered that Fauxnimal may have been begging to be shot as well. The song/dance already felt as though it was going to go on forever.

There's a skywalk that's twisted

It's got up and over bends

Goes doobie doo down down

Then homewards it wends

("Oh Sedaka" Griffin screamed)

Go on the run, past the pigpen,

That swirls with swine sweat

The porkers there will provoke you

The sows are coquettish croquettes

(Griffin burped!)

As Fauxnimal crawled towards Alex with outstretched arms Griffin ran over with a large purple cape with gold piping and a matching hanky. He draped the cape over Fauxnimal's shoulders and dabbed at his forehead with the piece of soiled cloth. He helped Fauxnimal to his feet but (to Alex's great disgust) it appeared his performance wasn't over. A series of knee drops, which caused to allway to thunder and echo like a storm in a box canyon, seemed to be an attempt to finally put the abalone into the puff pastry.

"Oh, son of a bitch!" Fauxnimal said, "I think he's gone on to the 13th floor."

ELISSA MCKEE

The Porkers'll beg for some lemons

Or overripe Clementines

They're just trying to con you,

Juicy slop will be fine

And when they start their sad oinking

Best get further away

The last guy hung around too long

And he was lunch the next day

Fauxnimal collapsed to his knees again as Griffin joined in with that awful noise he considered singing.

You're on the way to making a 13th floor plan

It's really there

It's truly somewhere

If you actually care

It may be up or down no one knows where the 13th floor can

Be is it over here?

Where's not exactly clear!!??!!??

Fauxnimal held a quivering quavering hovering hand up to Alex as though he was begging absolution for a life filled with lies, deceit and all around animus towards mankind. Alex was just about to reach out and take it when the singing began again. It was part of the performance.

'Damn!' thought Alex.

You'll reach the room full of mirrors
Where will it lead to this time?
Maybe a room with black curtains
I wish I had a white walls rhyme

You come to the master chamber
They serve shrimp cocktail on ice
They say they're only for members
The 13th floor's not really that nice

"Really?" said Alex aloud, "Won't this ever end?"

Fauxnimal and Griffin were really getting into it and they broke into an ultra hyper rhythmic rendition of the Colombian Boogaloo complete with airplane sounds, Guantanamo slip step, and the infamous necktie variation.

Just make an appointment
And back out through the door
You'll find yourself just outside
a passage to the 17th floor

You might think you're in heaven
You're really too close to tell
You're opposite of where you want to head
At the foot where our leadership smells

Fauxnimal reached up to Alex again. But he wasn't there.

"Oh, son of a bitch!" Fauxnimal said, "I think he's gone on to the 13th floor."

"It's really there," Griffin sang, "If you actually care!"

"Are the words 'shut' or 'up' in your vocabulary?"

"Up the stairs went Alex, and he quietly pulled the door shut behind him!" Griffin replied smugly.

"You're an idiot Griffin."

"Yes," Griffin told him, "but I'm still your immediate supervisor."

"You're right," Fauxnimal answered, "and someday monkeys will fly out of my butt."

A horrible sadness crept over Griffin's face and he began to cry out of each wandering eye.

"What's the matter now?" Fauxnimal asked.

"We never got to hear that part of the story."

And with that Fauxnimal smiled and began a cookin' re-do of the Colombian Boogaloo with a little hot buttered popcorn soul thrown in for good measure.

It anti-mattered.

N

CHAPTER 11EVEN:
THE 13TEENTH FLOOR

CHAPTER 11EVEN

Alex just couldn't stand there and stand it, so he'd walked away from the miserable noise being made by Roger and Rupert and entered the first door at which he'd arrived.

The CEO and Prince sat next to each other behind a seven by three foot table... what happened to the fourth foot was anyone's guess. Jonas Anyone, who wasn't important enough to be in this story until now, shouted "I bet it fell off!" Sure enough, there it was, on the floor, attached to the rest of the table leg.

The missing foot appeared to be causing quite a commotion for CEO and Prince. CEO couldn't get the hang of shuffling his papers at such a steep downwards slope and Prince's lipstick wasn't going on as planned. She could get the bottom lip to look somewhat feminine but the top marking spread all across her upper lip and made her look quite porcine.

"There you are!" shouted CEO, "There you are!"

He returned to his paper shuffling.

"Now," Prince said smacking her lips while grunting a few gray poofs of burp into the air, "where is the list!" That's when Alex noticed that the object of her stern words, acid release and lip slurps was Blanca.

"I um had it right here, just awhile ago, I don't know what…"

"You are FIRED!" shouted Prince smugly.

Blanca began to cry quietly, and Alex's heart sank in his chest, upsetting his stomach quite a bit when it hit bottom.

"You had a real future with RAW," Prince continued, "and now you've ruined it by not being able to carry out a simple task. I had big plans for you. But they are now past!"

"I had big plans for her too," said Griffin who'd somehow snuck into the room behind Alex, "but I couldn't get them through the doorway. One of them was a full sized diagram of a battleship which wasn't built because it turned out to be too large to fit on the planet. We talked about putting it into outer space but some idiot poo-poo'd the idea because they believe outer space is counterproductive."

"You're fired," screamed Prince.

Griffin's face sunk like Alex's heart, or his own battleship diagram, upon realizing that Prince was that poo-pooing idiot.

"I bet she lost the report that I didn't get to her in time for her to bring to this meeting!" Joe Fischer said with two parts disappointment and one part dejection in his voice. His nose hair seemed to agree with his conjecture.

A tiny woman with large ears and wispy whiskers protruding from her upper lip and chin ran her runny nose along her sleeve and said, "How can you be so…" before drifting off to sleep.

"Now you've gone and done it" said Matt, a tall man with a Y N on the front of his cap, "now you've gone and done it."

"Done what?" asked CEO looking up from his paper shuffling.

"It. Snot. She. It!" Matt answered.

"Then what is it?" the CEO asked but Matt didn't have an answer for that.

"Well I have some bad news for everyone!" The CEO said without looking at anyone. "Without that list we won't know who to layoff and who to layon. I'm going to have to let us all go, starting with me and Princess here."

"I've never heard of such a thing!" Prince screamed.

"Is there something in your ears?" CEO asked as she banged on the table and sent little purps of brown gas into the air which formed obscenities the likes of which have never been heard until now.

Rabferdaptlumpherump!

Schizenfurnkatelladiznee!

Poot!

"Well that's it I guess!" said the CEO.

"But what about the rest of us?" A voice filled the room from a speaker hidden behind a plastic plant that was hanging from the ceiling. Alex recognized the voice that of the man with the eye patch who was standing directly behind the tall man with the opposing eye patch in the glass room who enjoyed watching people eat lunch (or something).

"That's a stupid question," another voice said softly, "Tell them Alex W Bland is in the room."

"Alex W Bland is in the room," said the first voice.

"Then send him here immediately," CEO said with determination.

"No," said the tall one, "in the room with you."

A loud silence filled the room until Alex finally spoke up. "I'm, um, right here."

"You're late, you're fired," Prince screamed.

It was Fauxnimal who spoke up and said, "I don't think you can fire him you know."

"WHAAAAAAAAAAAAAAAAAAAAAAAAAAAAAAAAAAAAAAAAAAAT!"

"I think Fauxnimal's correct," said Matt in the hat, "you and the CEO were just let go by the CEO because Blanca lost the list of people who were to be let go."

"Meeee Owwwww," said Lujuria the Cat.

Someone shouted, "What do we do now?"

A silent loudness filled the room.

Alex heard a voice in his right ear and glanced to his left. "Caught me," said Chester, a new pork pie hat tilted rakishly over one eye, which was just as well because he was moving so fast Alex couldn't see the other one.

"Listen Alex," Chester continued, "I don't want to blow this whole gig but um, you gotta make a choice. You can save Blanca, get fired, get everyone re-hired and then watch them all get fired or you can stay hired let Blanca remain fired and watch everyone else lose their job while the board of directors rehires the CEO and everyone remains fired slash hired in some fashion or other."

Alex thought about it for a second before answering. He was suspicious because it was just about the best recommendation he'd ever heard from a consultant. "What makes you think I can do either?"

"Because," Chester said as he disappeared completely, "you've got the list in your pocket."

Alex remembered the paper he'd picked up off of the floor. He took it out of his pocket, looked it over, thought about everything he'd gone through so far, looked over at Blanca's still teary eyes and said, "You shouldn't fire Blanca, you should be promoting her!" He couldn't believe the silken depth and richness of tone he was projecting. Every eye and eye patch was upon him. The room was as quiet as a vacuum.

"Why?" a voice called out quietly.

Everyone looked around but the source was no where to be found. Alex noticed a small gray rat had drifted into a portrait of RAW's floundering father Billiam "Chris" Tollnacht, the man who'd risked everything and ultimately got what he deserved... which was the extreme humiliation of a lifetime panhandling with an old gray lady near a column of New York's greatest museum.

Or something akin to that.

"We talked about putting it into outer space but some idiot poo-poo'd the idea"

DENISE ANDERSON POORE

"Because," Alex told everyone, "she asked me to bring it up just in case she lost it while she was bringing it up."

Each person looked to the other… which took quite a while considering how many people were in the room and how long it took them all to believe it made sense.

When everyone had finally smiled at him (even Griffin, with a smile that appeared to be a frown to most people) he took the piece of paper and handed it to Blanca. She gave him a quick kiss on the cheek and then handed it over to CEO.

"WHY," he said, "there's nothing on it!"

A gasp went up around the room and didn't come down for quite a while.

"I guess we all get to keep our jobs!" he said gleefully. There was much dancing and rejoicing (even by Rejames, Jonas Anyone's best friend, a character who didn't make it into the story at all) and smiling and smacking and leaping and phaloomphing (in the best sense) and people were happy all around.

But none were quite as happy as Alex, because he'd finally remembered to call his brain back and it told him that he was in love. And the way that Blanca was looking at him it appeared that she was in love too.

"Now," proclaimed Prince while burping up her soul, "what's next on the agenda?"

And with that the CEO handed her an envelope which she opened with a slish of her fingernail. She removed the letter from inside and read aloud… it read…

"Now," proclaimed Prince while burping up her soul, "what's next on the agenda?"

MARC ALVAREZ

```
Yo,

I quit.
```

D

CHAPTER 12ELVE:
PERCHANCE TO DREAM

CHAPTER 12ELVE

"Well," Prince proclaimed loud enough for somebody down in the secret secretarial pool to hear.

"It appears," she continued, "at least one someone is going to lose their job!" Since there were no windows in the room not one of them cracked.

"Other than you?" asked CEO.

"Don't get started!" she exclaimed!

One of the non-existent windows shattered and the CEO (who's name, by the way, was Edmington Oliver the Firth– which meant he was somewhere between the first and the fifth), knowing what usually happened when someone shouted loud enough to break something that didn't exist, sat back down behind the tilting desk and shuffled a few more papers around.

To and fro.

Toothy and frown.

Frothy and twoon.

And all of those things.

It was easy to see E.O. didn't like where this was all headed. Right out the non-window towards the very real cement sidewalk below. Every head (along with their faces) snapped back to Prince's voice of volcanic vavoom volume when she said, "Where did this piece of entirely insolent insubordination come from?"

"The envelope?" Fauxnimal asked with a bit of a smirk and everyone chortled for a second or so until Prince's face contorted and constricted into a fangy visage full of vituperative venom only an executive viper resident could envision.

A hush fell over the room and it took a good few minutes for everyone to extricate themselves. It was a thick, muscular and foamy hush of the kind you see on silently breaking waves or hear from silently walking braves in TV westerns.

"There's going to be hell to pay, you betcha!" Prince was obviously very unhappy with the circumstances surrounding her miserable day and she obviously hadn't obtained enough hell to keep her life securely within the boundaries of its disorder. As a matter of fiction, she felt as though her personal hell was under siege and she had to do something bold to both fortify it and break through the mess of these circumstances.

No one else seemed to see the mess at all, considering they were all going to keep their jobs… at least for now.

She slowly scanned the room (including a glance down to see E.O. who was slipping a picture of her on a pony at age seven beneath a report entitled "People not to re-hire for any reason".

"I've lost my train of thought along with the closing parenthesis in the previous paragraph," she shouted while waving her arms as if she was conducting the room. "Where was I?"

There was a mass realization among those in the no-strings-attached section of the room that if Prince was a deli sandwich she'd have been dropped from the menu long ago. (And funny enough that's where her future nickname Imalas Neerg came from, even though that's for another Looking Glass Day at RAW.)

Alex glanced over at Blanca and could see turmoil etched upon her beautiful face. The t began at her left ear and resulted in her making a profound declaration that stunned everyone, "OH!" before racing to her right ear l.

Alex knew that after helping her with the layout list (it couldn't be a lay off list because there wasn't anyone on it (including Jonas): so it was obvious the company had decided to lay their financial emergency on someone else's doorstep… thus layout" He'd have to step in again, no matter how bad or confusion the grammar, punctuation and speling was become.

His actions were becoming very becoming. He recognized the slight tears welling up in her eyes. It was easy to see she was disinclined to tell lies of any sort. Even to help someone who'd just helped her fend off someone who was obviously helping themselves. Help. Help. Help. The slight tear in her right eye was named Indy and the one in her left Cision.

"It was me!" Alex said before he'd even realized it. He scanned the room and all eyes were upon him. Not only did that make him quite uncomfortable but forced the realization of what he'd just said deep into his head.

The hush that had previously fallen over the room now encircled everyone. Even Blanca held her breath. Alex walked over to the tilted desk and snatched the piece of paper from Prince's hand.

"Looks like I forgot to sign it!"

He scrawled his name across the bottom of the page with a flourish (a flourish of the kind they used to sell in the olden days of Rome… fountains with panache), took a deep breath and smiled widely.

"You're fired!" Prince shouted.

Everyone chuckled and the hush lifted and drifted away… up into the air vents and throughout the entire building. On every floor workers stopped working… before giggling, laughing, guffawing, snickering, chortling, chuckling, convulsing, cracking up, crowing like kookooclowns, grinning like hyuckhyenas, howling like merthmonkeys, roaring like laughlions, rolling in their comedycubicles, screaming like hoppybirds, shrieking like smileshriekers, snorting like bahhaabulls, splitting their sides like Fatty Arbuckle's pants, tittering like Bwian's wabble, whooping like a cawcawcrane. It had been some years since anything this wonderful and/or spontaneous had happened at RAW.

"You know," Alex began as people settled in for something like a soliloquy but more like an address. "I've been working here for longer than I care to admit and I guess I've been a little too focused on getting my pay check every week!"

"Every week?" said Matt in the hat to anyone who would listen, which was no one or everyone, it's hard to tell.

"And I've got to ask… at what point are we trading our days for a carrot on a stick? Someone has to be enjoying himself."

The gentleman scholar from the forward stood up and said, "I'll have nothing to do with this soliloquy!" but was shouted down by those who realized it was neither soliloquy nor monologue as a result of periodic interjections by people other than Alex. The gentleman sat back down and, humiliated, said, "carry on."

"At what point," Alex said while climbing to stand upon the tilted table, "are we just killing ourselves with repetition. Where every action we take means we have one less breath to give."

He fell off. It appeared his book of poetry he'd been given (titled (of all things) "Bright Side of the Sun") wasn't thick or voluminous enough to balance out a missing foot. The room was deadly silent. Even Prince kept her mouth tightly clinched.

"Does all this nonsense go all the way to the top?" Alex asked from the floor.

"Higher than the 13th floor?" Rupert asked as if there was no such thing… which was actually true but would just get in the way of this finale and the fact that's where this chapter is taking place.

"Are those whom are thought to be running this company living the same slow death as we, or are they laughing at us while enjoying the sweetness which each new day brings?"

The vaguely Shakespearian nature of his statement caused everyone to look over at the CEO who, upon realizing he was being talked about began to furiously shuffle papers.

"Well maybe that's a bad example," Alex continued, "but what I'm trying to say is... 'is showing up early, going home late, burning midnight oil, passing paper up and down 12 floors...'

"What floor are we on again?" someone asked.

'...spying on each other while we eat lunch...'

The intercom system roared to life...

"That's not happening here at RAW, no one has ever proven it and please ignore this announcement as it is not being made."

'...and reinventing whatever it is we do until we're not good at doing whatever the thing is that we have reinvented. Is it really the best way to spend a life?'"

Most everyone nodded, a few shook their heads. Realizing that they were in disagreement they traded a few nods and shakes until everyone agreed to nod, shake, nod and then nod again to give a kind of YES answer that still hedged its bets.

"It's not enough for me!" Alex kind of expected everyone to cheer at this point but everyone had tried to clap using only their right hands instead. They then paired off and attempted to clap again but it didn't work until they finally realized they had to face each other. Smiling and strangely empowered they applauded heartily.

Blanca leaned over and kissed him full on the lips. He turned, looked at the hundreds of eyes staring at him...

...and fainted.

Alex opened his eyes and looked around his office. What a strange dream. What a strange place he had been.

APRIL MOORE

Alex opened his eyes and looked around his office. What a strange dream. What a strange place he had been.

He gazed at the framed poster the company had put up on his wall that showed a sweaty runner going up a hill with the title DETERMINATION in bold block letters at the bottom.

He frowned at it. "What in hell is that supposed to mean anyway?"

Perhaps his nonsense made more sense than the nonsense the company had hung on the wall of his office to try and help him make sense of the nonsense they were asking him to do everyday.

He wiped sleep from his eyes, got up, and wandered down the hallway towards Blanca's desk. He reached into his pocket and fumbled with the gold button he'd found by the elevators. He wondered what he was going to say to her.

She was already there.

Or still there as the case may be.

He imagined her dreaming...

Of pools, rats and java... and outer spaces.

Of flowers and races and many strange places.

And all manner of person, both odd and absurd.

Where everything changed with the choice of a word.

He reached down and lightly tapped her on the shoulder. She slowly opened her eyes and upon seeing him, smiled. "Hi."

"Want to go get some lunch?"

She looked at the clock on her desk. It was 8:30 in the morning. "Sure," she said. He smiled back.

Starting tomorrow they'd both have new jobs.

He would write fantastic stories.

She would make them into movies that everyone would want to see.

They would be very happy.

ELDDIR

EHT

REWSNA

SI

TLAS DLO YTSURC A S'ENO

S'REHTO EHT DNA

A

TSURC DLO YTLAS

BRIGHT SIDE
OF
THE SUN

"A Collection of Incredibly Awful Poetry"

Cheer for the Wino Sleeping

Give me a W!

She shouted to me

One wintery Christmas Eve

W is for Wine

I is for Indigestion

No is for Never

Let him calm his innards

Or smile for once

Is not enough

Just not enough

Cheers!

Good Cheers!

Quiet Eve, Let him sleep in his box

Quiet Eve, Leave the bottle beside him

Quiet Eve, Let's go home to our warm fire

Look, that dog's eating his foot!

Cantaloupe Day

OH Sweet Jesus

It's cantaloupe day

And I've forgotten

Once again

How can I face the children?

How can I face the wife?

How can I face another winter?

Or the rest of my life?

when I arrive

empty arms

no Melons

no Lucky Charms

Oh Sweet JESUS

It's cantaloupe day

Lizard and the Fly

The lizard and the fly
Don't last too long together
And I bet you know why

The fly was a buzzin' in the lizard's belly
It was much too dark for him to tell, he
Was in deep
Was the fly

The lizard got indigestion like a dog
eating a bum's foot

The Cannibal Priest

The cannibal priest
ate only the boys
the girls were left for the others

He ate Tommy & Billy
& Chuck and Willy
& Ferdinan and all his brothers

He ate Carlos & John
& even DeShaun
& an entire boy scout choir

Some he ate raw
Some he ate stewed
Some he ate cooked in a fire

There was only one time
he regretted his crime
it was soon after he'd hurled

Up came a ribbon
and up came a sock
it seems that he'd eaten a girl

And the cannibal priest ate only the boys!

The tuna jumped into the boat
And to the fisherman said
"You'll never catch me,
I'm too smart"
And the fisherman speared him
stone cold dead
right through the head
And cut out his intestines
and heart
and other gooey bits
It's Tuna Time!

THE LIPS THAT DUCKS HAVE

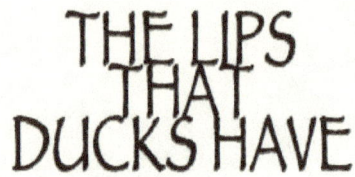

The lips that ducks have
are unlike any others
they are quite thin
and unburdened by feathers

they're water tight
just like at the ass
they're sharper than razors
or thin broken glass

they cannot be spit from
they cannot be pursed
they cannot be kissed from
they cannot be cursed

what they can do
hasn't yet been explained
but in sunlight they're chapped
and they're moist in the rain

oh how decidedly strange
are the lips that ducks have
really fucking strange
really really
            fucking strange

The president visited the Iraqi capital just
37 days before

a 39-year-old actress striped down next to
the headline:

Somalia's president attempts to oust prime
minister

Should Apple be boycotted because they
donated?

Despite mediocre reviews the film held fairly
steady

Take off your clothes 'til you're stark
raving nude

Our Litter Abatement Campaign represents a
citywide effort

When I was struggling to advance in the
business

The best way to do this is to copy and then
paste it

A music show, a talk show, a circus and a
therapy session

a master at the drums and in the kitchen

and some find love in being an ordained
minister

What's that smell?
Gerald shouted as
he took off his pants
Tina blushed and
pulled hers back on
Tuna Time had ended badly

WHAT IS THIS THING?

Often I am forced to ask
What is this thing?
You would think after a while
I could just say
I know what this thing is
But no
Know
I can't
I'm perplexed
And confused
And can't recognize
many of these odd amounts
of strange objects
which fall under the category
    "Things"
What is this thing?
You may ask
And you'd be right in doing so
I don't have a clue

This shall be the final poem
That you shall ever read
Until you move past it
Upon which that shall be the final
Poem you have ever read
And on
And on
Ad infinitum
Oh shit
Here comes more cut and paste…
"A 31-year-old real estate broker, was
accosted on a Brooklyn street by men who
yelled anti-Hispanic and anti-gay slurs"

nothing to see here
please keep moving
to the final poem
that you shall ever read

THIS SHALL BE
THE FINAL

Being out of Mayo
was never understood
by the people waiting in line
at the deli

Being out of Ketchup
was never tolerated
by the people who had
ordered up French fries

Mixing them together
was never desired
by the people who wanted
a salad

WHAT THE FUCK IS UP WITH CONDIMENTS THESE
DAYS...

WHY'S EVERYONE FUCKING WITH ME!

RUN LITTLE DOG!

```
Run Little Dog
Run    Run    Run

Don't eat that
Watch where you jump
Enjoy your nap
But not on the rug

Puke      Eat it!
Poo       Eat it!
Shoe      Chew it!
Chair     Chew it!

Scratch
Skritch
Itch Itch Itch

Knocking over the lamph
peeing on my amp
Butt scooting on the carpet
Humping Grandma's leg
```

```
Run
Little Dog
        Run
        Run
   Run
     Run
      Run
    Don't go into the STREET!
       STEW!
```

ONE LAST POEM

(THAT'S NOT SUPPOSED TO BE HERE)

This is that poem that is not supposed to be here and
I'm surprised it hasn't fallen back upon the little dog
...or perhaps after barking the little dog should slip
and slide and slop and go tumbling down into it!
Funny how life can be as mystifying as......
Letting someone sleep in a cardboard box
A hotdog ruined by ketchup (or catsup)
An elevator that never seems to stop
A building with no 13teenth floor
People who don't like cheese
A garden without flowers
Any love ending badly
A rat without a tale
A duck with lips
The banker who
worries about
his board of
directors
but not
about
this
w
o
r
l
d
And how a poem that isn't supposed to be here wants to be a tornado

...GOODBYE!

ABOUT THE AUTHOR

K. L. POORE
is a native of Southern California,
a place where he is the
only person who hates driving.

He's happily married
and has two Cats
(neither named Lujuria)
who are spoiled like
nasty thoughtless little children.

Periodically he can be found riding
buses around the Long Beach area,
talking to himself and strangers alike.

He'd like to acknowledge both
the Woodrow W. Poores (Sr & Jr)
for their incredible strength and
sense of unbounded silliness.
One of them continues to
make him laugh
to this very day.
The other one,
not so much.

www.ingramcontent.com/pod-product-compliance
Lightning Source LLC
Chambersburg PA
CBHW030502260626
47157CB00005B/1603